"So, Miss Carter." The attorney's tone was sarcastic. "So, you've written us a story. I see. Odd. The appellation of 'story'. It rather smacks of fiction, don't you think?"

"This one isn't fiction," Meg answered.

"Ah, but of course!" He nodded. "I imagine that's what every reporter says."

Then began an intense round of questioning. The paper's attorney wanted to know: Has Mr. Michael Gallagher ever been discussed in a public proceeding? Some legislative body sniffing out crime? Had he ever been arrested? Convicted? Could the son of a criminal public figure be regarded as a public figure himself? Had Meg done everything she could to ascertain the truth of her story—a story accusing Michael Gallagher of murder?

When he seemed satisfied, Meg asked, "Are you telling me to print?"

"I'm telling you madam, that the vaunted truth of your story is irrelevant. We are absent of knowledge that the story is false, therefore we are also absent of malice. We have done our very best and therefore we have not been negligent. So! We may therefore defame the man any way we like and he is powerless to harm us. Democracy is served."

COLUMBIA PICTURES PRESENTS

A MIRAGE ENTERPRISES PRODUCTION

PAUL NEWMAN   SALLY FIELD

ABSENCE OF MALICE

Music by DAVE GRUSIN

Director of Photography OWEN ROIZMAN, A.S.C.

Executive Producer RONALD L. SCHWARY

Written by KURT LUEDTKE

Produced and Directed by SYDNEY POLLACK

ABSENCE OF MALICE

A novel by Kerry Stewart

Adapted from the
motion picture
written by Kurt Luedtke

BALLANTINE BOOKS • NEW YORK

Library of Congress Catalog Card Number: 81-68644

ISBN 0-345-30161-7

Manufactured in the United States of America

First Edition: January 1982

DIAZ, Joseph A. See also Labor—Unions—International Dockworker's Union (IDU); Crime—Florida; Crime—Nevada.

U.S. Atty Harrison Quinn sets grand jury probe on waterfront crime. Cites mishandling of IDU funds., Joseph A. Diaz, pres Miami Dockworker's local 308, subpoenaed to testify; hearing set for Sept 11. (Aug 7, 34:2)

Joseph A. Diaz, pres Miami Dockworker's local, rept missing on August 10 when fails to return from afternoon swim; police find his car abandoned at beach; suspect foul play. (Aug 11, 1:4)

Miami and Florida State police, investigating disappearance of Diaz, focus on figures in organized crime. Informant says Diaz was waiting at beach for meeting with reputed Mafia leader S. Malderone; Malderone denies. (Aug 12, 1:2)

Police say Malderone's alibi checks; at Lauderdale Golf Club when Diaz vanished; witness is club-owner Franklin McKee, brother of union's nat'l pres Colin McKee. (Aug 14, 17:2)

FBI, under Federal statutes, begins investigation of Diaz abduction; Miami Special Agt Robert M. Keener slated as chief; Keener says former 308 pres Frank Cavaletti is possible key; said to have threatened Diaz's life and feared his appearance at grand jury probe; according to another reliable source, Diaz reptdly charged Cavaletti was "nothing but a no-good Mafia mole" who "loansharked the pension-fund money to hoods"; Keener will neither confirm nor deny. (Aug 16, 17:2)

Justice Dept Sp Atty Elliot Rossen, head of the Strike Force on Organized Crime, offers some theories on Diaz abduction: Diaz abducted by Frank Cavaletti, who may have embezzled or loansharked the funds; S. Malderone still under suspicion. (Aug 22, 17:3)

Sources close to investigation say evidence now reveals Colin McKee, nat'l pres IDU, was seen in Miami with S. Malderone the day before Joseph Diaz was nabbed; McKee tells *Washington Star*, "It's a lie." (Aug 27, 17:2)

Federal Agent Robert M. Keener admits possibility Diaz is dead; concedes "we're up against a big stone wall"; adds, "So was Joshua." (Aug 31, 23:2)

1.

"Dirty trick, Meg."

"What?"

"You wrote what I told you in bed."

"Where are you calling from?"

"Phonebooth."

"You want to come over and talk?"

"No. Was the whole thing a goddam hustle? Did you get into bed with me just for the quote?"

"No. For your body." She laughed abruptly. "Hey look, don't be mad. Hey listen, I thought you came off sounding good. I mean, listen, that line about Joshua? Jesus. You sounded heroic."

"Not to the Bureau."

"Oh."

"Uh-huh. Never thought of that, eh? Terrific. I'm two weeks onto the case and I'm publicly saying I'm up against stone. Only I didn't know it was public."

"Well . . . I'm sorry."

"No. You're not."

She was silent for a moment. Keener lit a cigarette. Looking through the phonebooth door to the lobby, he could see the insignia, seven feet high and hung on the wall: Justice—blind as a fucking bat.

"No," she admitted. "I was doing my job."

"For a second there, I thought you were doing something else." Keener heard the wounded tone in his voice and hated it.

"I'm sorry if I hurt you," she said.

"You didn't."

"Professionally."

"Oh." Keener took another drag of his smoke. "Gotta go. I got a meeting now at—"

"Keener?"

"What?"

5

"Please—I didn't have an ulterior motive. I *like* you. I wasn't doing what you think, and I'd *certainly*—"

"Then what are you doing tonight?"

"I'm busy. I've got this friend—"

"Then tomorrow."

"She's staying on my sofa. She's in from New York."

"Uh-huh."

"I'll call you. Maybe next week."

He suddenly laughed.

"What's funny?" she said.

"The twentieth century."

"What?"

"Never mind." Keener hung up. He stood for a moment, blowing a smoke ring, watching it rise.

When he got to the seventh floor conference room, just across the hall from the Strike Force office, it was empty. A giant windowless room—elliptical table, leatherette chairs—a room without character, history, air; a part of the brand-new Federal Building that was, Keener thought, one of Greater Miami's greater mistakes. He grabbed himself a chair at the end of the table, chain-lit a cigarette, stubbed out the butt, and counted up the number of times in his life he'd been an absolute schmuck.

Hamilton strolled in at number eleven. "Jesus. You know what Rossen wants now?"

"No. I'll bite. What does Rossen want now?"

"Shit, I don't know. I was asking."

"Cute."

"Cute." He sprawled in the chair next to Keener. "Jesus, the man's really out of his mind. You know that."

"I know that."

"He's out of his mind." Hamilton whistled, softly, drumming on the arm of his chair. "And I hear he's not exactly in love with you today."

"Almost nobody is."

"Were you drinking, or what?"

"The question, I believe, is 'were you drinking *again.*'"

"Were you?"

"No."

"Then you must be in love."

"Forget it. She's flat-chested, skinny—"

"And blond and blue-eyed and——"

"Right. Who needs it?"

Reagan came in, with Carroll, McArdle, and Bolt on his tail. He squinted from Keener to Hamilton. "Jesus. Your FBI in action," he said.

"Fuckups, Bureaucracy, and Inconsistency," Hamilton grinned at him. "How come you're here? You bust Malderone for a five-dollar bag?"

"Full-dress meeting, is all I was told."

"Shit. I'd've fully dressed if I'd known." Hamilton fingered the knot on his tie. Keener tipped his chair back and counted the house: the cream of the creamers, the Hot Turkey Squad. Represented in the room was the IRS, the DEA, the FBI, the Miami PD, the State PD. "And all the king's horses and all the king's men," Keener said softly.

Rossen came in, briskly, flanked by Mason (Bureau of Alcohol, Tobacco, and Firearms), and Dack (Department of Labor). Christ, Keener thought, everyone's here but the CIA. And the cavalry. Rossen didn't sit down. He stood for a moment at the head of the table, chewing at the inside wall of his cheek. He was thin, even paler than he usually was, and his hands, when he reached for a cigarette, shook. He wasn't sick; he was overwired. He reminded Keener of one of those inbred neurotic dogs— a Yorkie, forever yapping at heels.

He lit the cigarette now, turning to the side, the flame cupped deeply in the bowl of his hands, as though he were foxing a hurricane wind. He clicked off the lighter, a jet stream of smoke shooting straight from his nose. "And speaking of big stone walls," he began, "I think we'd do better to stonewall the press." He paused, shook the lighter around in his hand, rattled it—nervous crapshooter's move. "All right. On the other hand, the wall's really there. And unless we get lucky, we got it for good. To wit: we're being dicked around by the mob. Alibi Ike was with Alibi Mike, and everybody else was in Kalamazoo. Turkeys are frightened. Pigeons have flown. We got forty-six grand to buy talk on the street and we can't buy hello." He paused, looked around him. "So what do we know? We aren't moronic, so what do we know?" His black eyes buzzed over everyone's face like a pair of mosquitos. "We know Cavaletti. We know Malderone. We know they had motives, and so did McKee. Any number can play. Conspiracy? Maybe. Supposing it was. But all three together? Or two out of three. Or maybe it was one of them acting alone. Or *maybe*"—he buzzed at the faces again—"maybe it's someone we haven't considered. A 'foreign helper.' Does anyone happen to follow my drift?" He waited. Apparently nobody did. He nodded, a man one-up on the planet, and punched at the intercom.

"Charlie?" he said. "Go on. Let 'er roll."

The lights started dimming. Keener turned around and looked at the small projection-booth window at the back of the room.

"I discovered some interesting film," Rossen said. "Surveillance. It was taken in 'seventy-eight. In fact it was taken by Agent Keener."

Keener looked up. Academy leader was floating on the wall: . . . 9 . . . 8 . . . 7 . . . 6 . . . What the hell could be brewing in the man's little mind?

. . . 3 . . . 2 . . .

Hamilton laughed. "Christ. Tommy Gallagher's funeral."

"Shit."

On the screen now, a circle of two dozen mourners; a flashy coffin; a still-open grave. The film was a grainy black-and-white silent, but Keener could remember the chorus girl's wail, the priest, laying Gallagher into the ground, intoning the promise of a greener pasture, followed by what had to be a heavenly hedge: "All good men," he said, "go to heaven. And God, in His wisdom, will know who they are." The mourners could then believe that God in His wisdom would see beyond Gallagher's fleshier flaws to the virtuous spirit that dwelt underneath. Or not.

"Tommy Gallagher," Rossen announced. "Bootlegger, loan shark, high-rolling gambler. After Prohibition he called himself—get this—'liquor importer.' Owned himself a warehouse. Down by the docks."

On the screen now, the camera was framing the priest, who lifted his hand in what appeared to be a blessing but was actually a move meant to cover his face. The circle of mourners broke from the grave and Keener—who'd been standing there holding the camera, uninvited and undisguised—had narrowed his lens on the scattering crowd.

"Cavaletti," Rossen said. "Just look at that bastard. Mink-collared coat. Headed the local here for thirty-six years. 'Lent' Tommy Gallagher close to a mil. Pension-fund money. Debt never paid. And there goes McKee. And watch it—on the left now—*there*—there he comes. The Godfather. Santos 'The Eel' Malderone. In heroin circles, he's King of the Keys. In spirit, he's Cavaletti's employer. In fact, Tommy Gallagher's brother-in-law. Okay. You guys see why we're screening this?"

"Sure," Reagan said. "You want to see Keener get punched in the jaw."

"And here comes the puncher. Watch him now. Michael Anthony Gallagher. Age forty-seven. Dig: Tommy Gallagher's only begotten. Malderone's nephew. 'Liquor importer.' And watch him move out."

Keener was wincing.

"Duck!" Reagan said.

"Fuck." Keener laughed now. "Well, what the hell."

Gallagher punched him. The camera jerked; it tumbled, then took a few pictures of grass. The screen went to black.

"That's it," Rossen said.

The room lights were up.

"Okay, so he did a few months in the slam, but we never really nailed him. Word is he's clean. I don't buy it," Rossen said. "Not for a second. He inherited the warehouse when Tommy kicked off. Let's figure he inherited some other things too. Like Tommy's little habits. Like playing potsie with Frank Cavaletti. Like saying 'uncle' to S. Malderone."

"Hold it," Carroll drawled. "I just want to get it straight. Are you makin this fella here a suspect or what?"

Rossen looked up. "Officially? No. Unofficially? Let's say I want him checked out. From cellar to belfry. I want to know everything there is on this guy." He pointed at Bolt. "Start with his taxes for the last seven years."

"*Seven?* C'mon! I mean, Christ, he's only been in Miami for three."

"All right. So we'll split the difference, okay? Six,"

Rossen said. "And as long as you're up, you can do it like you're doing me a net-worth case. I want to know every nickle he's got and where he got it. And then I want to know where he's spending it, right? So talk to his banker, talk to his broker, talk to his tailor, talk to his goddam travel agent, talk to his anybody-else-you-can-think-of . . . except for his lawyer. Okay. Moving on—

"Peter? You guys take his labor stuff, right? I want to know exactly how he deals with the unions, especially how with the IDU. Mason? He's wholesaling liquor and wine. Be sure that it's kosher."

"You're kiddin. The *scotch?*" Mason hooted. "Hey Bob, you ever hear of any kosher—"

"No no no," Rossen cut in, frowning. "No jokes, no jokes. Just be sure what he's dealing is bonded and stamped. Check with his customers."

Mason looked up. "Well now, that's gettin kinda rough, ole buddy. That could put him out of business."

"Gee," Rossen said. "And I'd really lose sleep. Someone put *Diaz* out of business, remember?"

"Yeah," Mason said. "But I could check at the warehouse. Don't you think—"

"No! I think this is how you do it."

There was silence.

Hamilton eyeballed the ceiling.

Keener lit a cigarette and squinted through smoke. Rossen had turned to him. "Robert? The rest of this clambake is yours. Friends and neighbors, lovers and foes, employees, uncles—especially uncles. I want to know exactly where Gallagher stands. And I want to know exactly where Gallagher sleeps, and exactly where he was the day—"

"Whoa!" Keener said. "So far you got us talking to half of Miami."

"So?"

"So—it won't exactly stay quiet."

"So?" Rossen lifted his eyes to the room. "Any other objections?"

2.

It was not a good day. It had started with the phone-call: Keener, waking her; tart accusations on an empty stomach. ("Dirty trick, Meg.") She'd hung up the phone and then stared at the ceiling. ("Dirty trick, Meg.")

Well . . . . it wasn't. She'd interviewed him maybe a half dozen times—about Diaz, and before, on the Rutherford case. That was it. So she hardly knew the man, really; and certainly she owed him nothing at all.

She'd found him completely unimpressive at first; he was tall, very tan, but decidedly stiff. His eyes were a hard, incurious gray and his clothes were awful, somber and cheap; he looked as though he'd borrowed them for somebody's funeral. Keener. She'd dismissed him as Typical Fed, no keener than most, but then she'd been surprised by the flashes of wit, delivered with the straight expressionless face, and that genuine toughness she'd seen in his eyes. She admired toughness, physical as well as intellectual grit. A man who could fight could take care of himself—or her—if the situation ever arose, and she felt an almost envious attraction to that. Or at least to the attribute of toughness itself.

On Wednesday she'd been sitting in the R & R Bar, an after-work hangout, when Keener came in. He was there with his partner and they'd sat in a booth, talking, and she'd noticed he was drinking a Coke, and she'd sent him a note that said, "This is a Coke bust. You're under arrest." She'd been there with Alicia, who'd left around eight, and then Keener had stayed. They'd talked ("No comment on Diaz," he'd said) and then gone for a burger and gone for a ride and then walked on the beach—him in his goddam wingtip shoes. Still, in the moonlight, he'd seemed if not clearly, then obscurely handsome; his mouth appeared pleasant and invitingly wry. And later, when she'd asked him to come up for a drink, he'd shrugged and said, "Yeah, if you make the drink coffee," and—

11

they'd talked over coffee, talked lightly, nothing serious, and then went to bed.

Where Keener got serious.

It wasn't exactly anything he said, it was just how he acted. His tenderness frightened her. His expectation was written in his eyes, and she'd thought, oh, Jesus, I've made a mistake.

And then, in the morning, she wrote what he'd said. Why not? His admission was page-one stuff—except it got shunted onto page 23 because who could know a nut would take a shot at the mayor. But anyway, the point was, she told herself now as she walked up the steps to the Federal Building, he'd said it to her knowing full well who she was. She'd used no deception; she'd used no disguise. It was true, she'd brought up the subject of Diaz, but that's all she'd done. It was Keener. He'd simply blurted it out; blew it out with *après* cigarette smoke. His error. Not hers.

And to hell with it.

Or . . . not that easy.

She stopped in the lobby and looked at her watch; it was ten to eleven. All right, so she could cover the action in court and then mend a few fences—"smooth things over," as her father would say. Her job had been rough enough going as it was—the erratic beat of the Federal Building: the courts and the famous alphabet soup of the FBI, IRS, DEA, etc., and no one ever promised it was duck soup, either. The agencies never said a goddam thing, except for the canned "investigations-in-progress-are-a-government-secret." End of report. End of reporter. If you wanted a story, McAdam advised her, you had to be willing to dig and connive, and Meg had uncloaked a real talent for digging; she'd hit a metallic vein in her soul. At first she'd observed it with a sense of elation, Eureka! as though she'd discovered her truth. But then came the snag-toothed bite of her conscience (Connecticut Yankee in Federal Court) and the feeling that she wasn't entirely . . . well, . . . nice.

And to hell with that too.

Her job would go better if she straightened things out. And besides, if she convinced Keener she was innocent, she might, without further debate, convince Meg.

Damn fucking Yankee conscience, she thought.

The Bureau's Division of Organized Crime was a couple of squadrooms at the end of a hall. Keener had a cubicle in one of the rooms. The cubicle was empty.

Meg cleared her throat.

Donna Bellinsky looked up from her desk. Donna was forty, with short black hair, and the adjective generally applied to her face was "friendly," which didn't apply to it now. She shook her head slowly and tch-ed with her tongue. "Naughty, naughty."

Meg made a face. "I take it I'm persona non grata today."

Donna shrugged. "If I knew what that meant— But I think you've been declared off limits to the troops."

"Oh."

"In fact, they're putting out a training film on you."

"Oh Christ," Meg laughed. "Are you mad at me too?"

"Hell, no. You're just playing the game like the boys. You're playing your game, and Bob's playing his. And I can tell you this, cutie, I've been secretary here now for twenty-two years and I'll tell you: he could take you to dinner or bed, but he'd bust you like *that* if you were into something crooked. Count on it."

"Right."

"It's a big-league game."

"I guess."

"Don't guess. It's a big-league game. Hardball, Meggie. Watch out for the curves."

"Thanks."

"Hey, for what?" Donna plucked a lit cigarette from the ashtray and puffed on it. "Ask me, I think you did wrong. I mean, why'd you have to go on and blab it was Keener? How about 'sources high in the sky'?—or however you guys always say it."

"I tried."

"But?"

"But my editor said it was vague."

"Well I say it's lousy."

"Is he really in trouble?"

"Keener? Got yelled at, if that's what you mean. He'll

survive. Hey, look, he didn't give you the Pentagon Papers. He just said the obvious."

"True," Meg agreed. "Where is he, do you know?"

Donna looked up. "No place you'd care about. They're all at the movies."

"Wait. Don't tell me. *The FBI Story* with Jimmy Stewart."

"Nope. With Keener, as a matter of fact. Surveillance film. Tommy Gallagher's funeral. Figure the screening's El Rossen's revenge."

"Meaning?"

"Meaning Keener gets clobbered at the end. Rossen only strikes by proxy. What a creep!" Donna leaned forward and waggled her pen. "And let me tell you, *there's* the guy who took the story hard. Doesn't like it mentioned when he's falling on his face. You should have seen him this morning. Pacing the decks and rolling little marbles, like Captain Queeg."

"Who's Tommy Gallagher?"

Donna shook her head. "He's no one. A long-dead mobster." She grinned. "No story in that. Believe me now, cutie, I wouldn't tell you anything remotely useful."

"Thanks." Meg smiled. "Tell Bob I was here?"

"Sure. Any messages?"

"Yeah. Tell him— No. Just tell him I came to say hello."

The telephone rang. Donna answered it; Meg waved good-bye and walked out.

In the corridor, she stopped just beyond the doorway, noticing a quarter that was lying on the floor, and heard Donna say, low, "The Gallagher file? You're kidding! But I thought— Never mind. I'll get it. Yeah. Okay."

Meg picked the quarter up, thinking it had to be a piece of good luck.

3.

"What's your game, Elliot?"

Rossen looked up. This time his hand toy was a big rubber band. A red one. He stretched it from the tip of his thumb to the raised middle finger of his opposite hand. A sling. He aimed it at a fictive Goliath. Or the window. "Gallagher. Gallagher's the game." He shot; the rubber band went thwonk, hit the floor. "I'm the hunter, okay?"

Keener just nodded. "Then let me put it this way. Why the hell are you hunting him with T-54s?"

"With what?"

"With tanks," Keener said. "Big fucking unsubtle sixty-ton tanks."

Rossen said nothing; he plucked another red rubber band from his pocket and twiddled it.

Keener said, "Look: for the record. My jaw and I aren't any fans of this guy. Okay? I'll even buy that he might have had a motive, or a friend who had a motive—"

"Or both," Rossen said. "How about a friend who might've gave him the contract. He's a sharpshooter."

"Is he?"

"Oh yeah. It's in the record. Look, I want to question this bastard, all right? But before we question him, I want to know exactly what to question him about. I want to know what kind of leverage we've got. What dirt we could promise him immunity for. If we have to."

"So you don't think he did it."

"Maybe. I don't know. I mean, shit, I wouldn't give him immunity for *that*. But I'd like to go in and say, 'Okay, fella. We got you dead for twenty-seven counts of playing smartass. Talk or take jail-time.' That's what I'd like."

"That and a yellow Maserati for Christmas. What if he doesn't know anything to talk about. Then what?"

"He knows."

"God talks to you? How do you know that he knows?"

"Hunch." Rossen settled his head on the doorknob. "Hunch. Like my hunch about the Rutherford case. Was I right about that or was I right about that?"

Keener said nothing.

"It's worth looking into."

"But quietly, Elliot. On little cat feet."

"Cat *shit*. I want Tommy to *know* we're in town."

"Tommy?"

"Mike. Mike. Put him under surveillance. A hot surveillance."

"I don't think so."

"What's that supposed to mean?"

"It means that's classified as harassment, Elliot. It also means I work for the Bureau, not you. Remember? I report to Shiloh, not you. And Shiloh won't buy it."

"You mean you won't sell it."

"And I won't sell running in with noisemakers either."

"But I'll win that."

"Probably," Keener admitted. "We'll see."

Rossen stood. "Nice talkin to you, kiddo."

"You weren't," Keener said. "I was talkin to myself." He stood. "And I said to myself, holy shit! If we go in like gangbusters all over town, what could happen to this guy if he *does* know something? And I said to myself, this guy could get killed."

"Yeah," Rossen said. "Yeah, well I'll put it on my worry list, kid. Bottom of page ninety-seven."

He aimed, and shot Keener's shoe.

Back in his office, Keener checked with Donna. "Anything?"

"A guy named Rasmussen called. He said don't call him."

"*Don't?*"

"Don't."

"Right," Keener nodded. "Anything else?"

Donna looked up. "Your pen pal was here."

"You're funny," Keener said. "What the hell did she want?"

"Absolution, I think."

"Don't we all," Keener said.

At his desk, he picked up the phone to call Shiloh, considered the futility, and put the thing down. He wasn't in any position to complain. Rossen had been in to see Shiloh this morning and, according to reports, suggested that rusty nails be left around for Keener to step on. Lockjaw being the hoped-for result. That or get a muzzle, Rossen had said, and Shiloh had agreed. Therefore anything Keener said today would be interpreted as spite. He knew Shiloh's mind; it was one of those small ones, and Shiloh liked to keep it tidy and clean. Once he'd made it up for the day, it was made. If Keener was wrong, he was wrong all day, and there was nothing he could do about it.

Shrugging, he reflected on chains of command and how they were sure as hell chains, all right. Grabbed you by the ankle, kept you in line; jerked you in the kind of idiot directions that are led by a jerk.

I was a fugitive from a chain of command.

He lit a cigarette and fought back the craving he'd been fighting for months.

Rossen wanted Gallagher.

Keener wanted a drink.

Meg stopped in a phonebooth.

If you wanted to background a dead body, the best place to start your search was the morgue. She dialed.

"Library."

"Jimmy? Hi. It's Meg Carter here."

"And what can I do for you, Meg 'o my heart?"

Jimmy McCracken was seventy; fat. He'd once been a damn good reporter; thin. On his wall was a picture of McCraken, thin, covering the *Quinte Brigada* in Spain. He now ran the morgue at the *Chronicle-News*.

"Do we have any clippings on a guy named Gallagher? Tommy Gallagher?"

McCracken laughed. "Do we have any clippings on a guy named Capone?"

"Are you saying—"

"I'm saying, sure, we got clippings. You want 'em?"

"Please. He was bigstuff, huh?"

"Oh, that he was."

"Do you know how he died?"

"In bed. With a redhead. At seventy-eight," McCracken said. "Shit."

"My dime's about up. Can you have it on my desk?"

"Babydoll, the last time I had it on a desk was in nineteen thirty, but I'll sure as hell try."

"You know what I mean."

"Did you have to say that?"

"Sorry," Meg laughed. "And thank you."

"Good-bye."

4.

GALLAGHER, THOMAS EDWARD

Meg spread the open file on her desk. Most of the clippings were yellowed and brittle. The first time Gallagher's name appeared in any given clipping it was circled in red. It seemed to appear in the headlines a lot. Tommy Gallagher was headline stuff. She opened a carton of vanilla yogurt and studied a newsclip from 1920.

Gallagher was handsome, in a bluff kind of way. There was something that was almost sincere about the face. It was the face of a con man. Or a politician.

She skimmed the clippings with a speedreader's eye and picked up the story:

He was a bootlegger.

Indicted, but not convicted.

Indicted again, but not convicted.

Convicted, but appealed.

Won.

He played poker with Arnold Rothstein.

He also played poker with Nick the Greek.

He also owned a yacht that could take him to Cuba where he also broke the *banco* at the Casa de La Paz.

He was married to Maria Seraphina Malderone.

(Interesting. Only he was nonetheless dead.)

He was in a car accident.

He was in a boat accident: he was caught in a storm by the U.S. Coast Guard with two hundred cases of untaxed rum. They raided his warehouse on Pier 17.

Indicted.

Convicted.

Served four years in jail. From 1950 to 1954.

Took the Fifth Amendment—fifty-seven times—at a grand jury hearing on organized crime.

Again indicted (in '72) in a kickback scheme involving Frank Cavaletti.

Indictment overturned.

Died.

Meg sucked on a ballpoint pen.

Died.

Alive, he could well be a suspect.

Dead, he could only be a three-year-old corpse.

Question: So why is El Rossen's Strike Force developing an interest in a three-year-old corpse?

Answer: El Rossen is losing his mind?

No; that's a question.

Okay. Here's another one.

Question: They're screening his funeral film?

No; that's an answer.

Maybe.

Maybe.

Maybe they aren't interested in Gallagher but something that happened at his funeral.

Swell. Then why are they looking at his goddam *file?*

Unless . . . unless . . . it's not connected to Diaz?

No; I don't think so. No. El Rossen's obsessed with the case.

Funeral.

She flipped to the end of the file.

> **TWO-FISTED FRACAS AT**
> **GALLAGHER FUNERAL**
>
> ———————————
>
> **Son Socks Fed; Gets**
> **Hauled Off To Jail**
>
> ———————————

Son.

Son?

> . . . apparently irate at the obvious surveillance, Michael A. Gallagher punched the unidentified federal . . .

GALLAGHER, MICHAEL ANTHONY

Three clippings only.

He lived in New York. Or at least he'd lived there in '71. And the only clipping there had to do with a boat. A boat that he'd built. The boat was a racer and the race had been lost when the boat flipped over. The article mentioned, rather cutely, she thought, that Michael was the son of one Thomas Gallagher, "reputed Miami Mafia boss," who also had lousy luck with his boats. End of report.

Caption: GALLAGHER DREAMBOAT SUNK.

Picture: Gallagher. And even in the grainy newspaper print, and even all wet, he was something: a winner, grinning and shrugging.

Item #2 was the TWO-FISTED FRACAS.

Item #3 was GALLAGHER RELEASED.

Picture: Gallagher, glaring at the camera.

Caption:

Michael A. Gallagher, son of reputed Miami mobster, released from jail after 14 months.

There was no article, no explanation of why he'd served time. The picture was dated 6/27/79.

If the feds were looking at the Gallagher file, it had to be the Michael A. Gallagher file. Probably. Tommy didn't seem to have a brother or any other children.

Question: Did Michael A. live in Miami?

The phonebook was mangled and jammed between bookends at the center of her desk.

Michael A. Gallagher. Abingdon Place.

There was also a listing for Gallagher's Warehouse. Liquor Distributors. Pier 17.

So.

She grinned, and then let out a sigh.

So . . . what?

It meant nothing at all.

In terms of publication, what the hell could she say?

"Late this afternoon, unreliable sources, entirely removed from the investigation . . ."

No. She'd have to do better than that.

"Megan Carter, federal courts and agencies reporter for the *Chronicle-News*, reported, on early Friday afternoon that 'something was probably, maybe going on.' Carter, 27, both new to Miami and new to the job, drew on her extensive personal experience as a weather reporter

for Channel 13 to conclude, from a hint she picked up
with a quarter . . ."

McAdam looked at her. "That, and a quarter . . ."
She nodded. "I know."
"What else have you got?"
"I don't even have that."
McAdam said. "Hmp." He added, "Hur*ummm*."
McAdam had been weaned on the kind of old movies
where tough city editors hmphed and hurummmed. Mc-
Adam was fifty and glad that he was. He remembered
when newspaper writing was a game (The Newspaper
Game); not Journalism, Bastion-of-Democracy, Truth,
Voice of the American Conscience, but *fun*. Good old,
plain old muckraking fun. He resented the rulings of the
managing editor, but followed them, knowing how a job
was a job, and how McAdam was fifty and not in de-
mand.
McAdam looked up. "What else don't you have?"
"I don't have the reason they're investigating Gallagher
. . . *if* they're investigating Gallagher."
"Right. So when can you get it?"
"I don't think I can."
"Sure you can. Quinn. How about Quinn? Can you
work him? He wants us to love him this week."
"As a mayoral candidate."
"So? Approach him as a mayoral candidate. Tell him
we want to do a profile, right? Promise him anything,
give him our page, but slip in the question: 'Oh, by the
way . . . ' "
"Mmm. But the thing is, I'm not sure he'd know. I
mean, Quinn's the D.A., but Rossen runs the Strike Force.
And Rossen hates Quinn. And he doesn't have to tell
him—"
"Which leaves us with Rossen."
"With whom we could be left on a desert island for
several decades and not get a word."
McAdam thought it over. "All right. Okay, So you're
back to square one."
"Which is?"
He grinned. "The one square you know: Keener."
"Forget it. Not now. He wouldn't give me the time from

my own watch, thanks to you. You really bitched me up with that dumb attribution."

"Me?" McAdam said. "Not me. That was Managing Edwards who did it. Do I give a shit? Listen: this was back in—Jesus, it must've been in nineteen-fifty. I was working in Washington. Story was a thing about a military clerk. He's spying for the Ruskies, something like that. So anyway, I'm talkin to this other clerk, see, and he's givin me all kinds of bullshit and blather, so anyway, I said to him, 'Charlie, c'mere,' and I take him in the elevator, take him to the roof, and then I call him 'sources high in the Pentagon.' Shit!" McAdam laughed. "Do I give a shit?"

"No," Meg nodded. "I can't get to Keener."

"Sure you càn. You want to make the *New York Times*?"

"You know I do."

"Visit him with big limpid eyes. Turn on the old Farrah-Fawcett of charm. You tell him you're sorry. You blame it on me. Then you kind of worm it all out of him. Con him. Get the information any way you can, only get it. I'll let it go without attribution."

"And then what?"

"And then you quit the *Chronicle-News* and go off with your clippings and dazzle the *Times*. If you mean what we do about the damn attribution, I think it's 'Reliable sources today—' "

"Them again. Listen, it's Friday today."

"So?"

"I don't know if I can reach him today."

"So try it. Okay? God loves a trier."

"Yeah." Meg nodded and walked to her desk.

The telephone caught him in the middle of a shower. Cursing, he dripped to it. "Keener," he said.

"Oh, Keener," she laughed at him. "Keener. Is that the way you answer in your *house? 'Keener'?"

He fumbled for a cigarette, wet, and found he was pulling on a wet cigarette; the thing wouldn't light. "What's on your mind?"

"What's on your schedule?"

He tried another match. "Work."

"On a Sunday?"

"Yeah," he said sharply. "I'm really a constant hilarious surprise, aren't I? The dumb way I answer my phone? The days that I work?"

"I'm sorry," she said.

"That's hilarious too." He grabbed another cigarette. "Listen, Meg, I'm standing here on two hours' sleep, so if I sound a little testy—"

"How about a nice, relaxing little brunch?"

Keener said nothing.

"Hey, c'mon, Keener. Give yourself a break."

He grunted. "I guess."

"Then how about Tasco. Quarter of one?"

5.

The restaurant was done up to look like a patio; red tile flooring and fat potted palms. She was late; she didn't honestly mean to be late, but she was. He was sitting there, waiting at the bar with a dumb Coca-Cola. He was wearing a suit. His copper-color hair had been cut—too short. But then when she was next to him, heading for a booth, he offered her the faintest aroma of lime and she could picture him, standing at his bathroom sink, splashing his face with some lime-colored glop. For a moment she almost felt guilty as hell.

He shrugged and said, "So. You called."

She nodded. "I wanted to explain."

"Forget it."

"I can't. Hey, listen, what I wanted—"

"Hey, I *know* what you wanted. What you wanted was to push me away and you did. Message received. So the question on the table now is, what do you want?"

For a moment she was much too stunned to reply.

He grinned at her. "Well. You've been thrown off your guard. That's nice." He picked up the menu and looked at it, nodding. "Spanish. Spanish," he said. "What I really need now is a Spanish breakfast."

When the waiter walked away, she said, "Why did you come?"

"For the Spanish omelet."

"Why?"

"For the Spanish Inquisition."

She sighed.

"I was testing, I guess."

"Me?"

"Me."

"Oh," she said lightly. "Well, you're doing just fine."

"Yeah. For a defensive tackle, I am. I don't think I feel exactly safe with you."

"Oh."

25

"I mean it. You're the worst kind of dangerous, Meg. You're careless. You're a rookie with a shiny thirty-eight and you're either gonna shoot the whole room or your foot." He looked at her. "I mean that as a general comment. Not about . . . anything that happened with me." He squinted. "And I think that's probably a lie, but only a half one."

She looked at him slowly with her head to the side. She smiled. "You're really very likable, you know?"

"Bullshit. I said something highly instructive just now, and you missed it."

The waiter came back. "Platter of tacos, two bowls of chili." He grinned, putting platters and bowls in their place.

Keener said, "Another Coke for the lady and a vodka for me."

Frowning, the waiter said, "The other way around?"

"Right," Keener nodded. "The other way around." He played with his Coke glass and looked up at Meg. "I'm waiting," he said.

"For what?"

"I don't know. For the first shoe to drop." He shrugged. "I guess I'm waiting to hear what you want."

"Can I ask you a question?"

"About?"

"About you."

"Me? I'm obvious."

"Are you?"

"Not when I don't want to be, no."

She thought about that. "Have you worked under-cover?"

"Sure. Under yours."

She flushed. "Be serious."

"Babydoll, that's the whole problem. I was."

She stared at her chili.

"I worked in Chicago. I worked undercover."

"As?"

"Clark Kent. Same thing as now. I'm really a daring, pot-smoking pimp. This is my cover."

"Okay. I'll give up."

"I worked counterterror."

"Did you?"

"Uh huh."

"Fascinating."

"No. Maybe. I don't know."

She looked at him. "What do you mean, you don't know?"

"*You* know, right?" He laughed, but she noticed his fist; it was clenched; he reached for his Coke.

She decided it was time to make a change in direction. and she told a few stories and watched him relax. Then she told a really funny little anecdote, something that had happened at a party last May, only she pretended it had happened last night. He laughed, and she said, very cooly, "By the way . . . this friend of mine—the girlfriend who's in from New York? Well, she met this kinda good-looking guy at the party. Michael Gallagher, I think was his name. And the thing is, I wondered if . . ."

"Shoot," McAdam said.

"I tried. I think what happened is, I shot my own foot."

"Nothing?"

"Got stared at with cop-blank eyes."

"Nothing?" McAdam repeated.

"Exactly. In fact that's the only clue I really got."

"*Nothing?*" McAdam repeated, squinting.

"Exactly."

"You want to explain that?"

"No."

"Explain that," McAdam bellowed.

"Right. Well, the thing is I told him this girlfriend of mine was attracted to Gallagher. That part was fine. I mean, Gallagher's this really terrific-looking guy but anyway, I *seemed* to recall he was Mob, so I asked, for my friend's sake, was Gallagher clean."

"And?"

"He said he didn't have any idea."

"I see," McAdam nodded. "And that was a clue?"

"So then I asked if Gallagher ever did time."

"And he said he didn't know."

"Exactly. But he offered to check the computer."

"I see."

"You don't. Because Keener knows goddam well he did time, because Keener was the guy who busted him!"

"Was he?"

"Well . . . I'm not exactly sure about that, but I think so. It figures. Gallagher clobbered Keener at a funeral, and eighteen months later he's getting out of jail."

McAdam just looked at her.

"Listen," she said, "it's the best I could do."

McAdam shook his head. "I had faith in you, Megan. I really thought you had the old Donovan touch."

"Who's Donovan?"

"Mariah Donovan. Famous reporter. Hid in the bath-tub of a Marriott hotel room for seventeen hours while a congressman boffed his sweetie next door. For seventeen hours she listened to screams, hollers, moans, and the cracking of whips, and the whispered confessions to three counts of fraud. Her spine has the permanent shape of a bathtub, but Mariah was gutsy, Mariah was game."

"So what did you expect me to do?" Megan said.

"To learn what's cooking."

"So what did you expect me to do?" Megan said. "Hide in his oven?"

"Ply him with scotch. Fumble around in the old Bureau drawers. *I* don't know what."

She felt herself flush. "You're disgusting," she said.

"It wouldn't be the first time."

"Right. You're disgusting almost daily," she said.

"What I meant was, it wouldn't be the first time a woman—"

"Well, I wouldn't."

"Well, I didn't think that you would. I was joking."

"Oh."

"So go check it out."

"Check what?"

"Was Gallagher busted by Keener."

"And then what? I'm still left with nothing to print. Goddamit, McAdam. This story is true. I know it."

"Then try it on Rossen or Quinn."

"I guess."

"But go in to them armed with conviction."

"Gallagher's?"

"Right."

6.

The Department of Records in the Federal Courthouse was a giant air-conditioned barn of a room. The clerk was a lumpy middle-aged woman with carroty hair who'd bundled herself up in a piled cardigan. Mrs. Greavis, the placard said, and Mrs. Greavis could not be hurried, hustled, or charmed.

Three hours later Megan emerged with a headache, a chill, a half page of notes, and the certainty that Gallagher, Michael A., had been tried and convicted in Federal court on charges of assaulting a federal officer, January, 1978, and been sentenced to fourteen months in the slam. The clobbered Fed had been Robert Keener; the charges had been pressed by the Bureau itself; and the sentencing judge had been Carlton Mathis, otherwise known as Maximum Mathis, on account of his penchant for maximum terms.

Therefore, Keener had lied in his teeth.

Therefore, the Bureau was investigating Gallagher—nephew of Santos "The Eel" Malderone, and possibly connected, just like his daddy, to Frank Cavaletti and IDU funds.

Logical.

All it required was proof.

"Meg?" Eddie Hamilton tapped her on the shoulder. He was Keener's partner; a hustler, maybe ten years younger than Keener, and faster, looser, a whole different breed, with his shaggy black hair and his well-tailored clothes. "What's the matter?" he said. "You get locked out of Quinn's little conference, or what?"

She cocked her head at him. "What conference?"

"Quinn. Announcing he's running for mayor. Ta-*da!*"

She nodded. "As if we didn't know."

"Jesus, I seen him kiss a few babies, but I figured it's just cuz he's a dirty old man."

She laughed. "Well, I wouldn't get invited there anyway. That's Ammico's beat. Politics."

"Yeah. What isn't these days."

She looked at him.

Hamilton lifted his shoulders. "You should watch him. His footwork's faster than a roach. The Committee for a Better Miami's endorsing him, right? And you sure know what *they're* all about. Christ. What they mean by Better is whiter, and no *hablar* with the *espanol*. But you listen to Quinn try to have it both ways. He was in with this guy from *La Prenza* before, and I swear to God he's practically *smiling* in Spanish—*Hasta la vista*."

"And *buenos Diaz?*"

Hamilton grinned. "I think that's a subject he'd rather avoid."

"How's it going?" Meg said. "Diaz, I mean."

"*Bueno*. It's always *bueno* to you."

"Working hard these days?"

"Always."

"Want to take a break for some coffee?"

"Nah. I can't. Thanks, though. Even if you do want to pump me, I'm flattered."

"It never entered my mind."

"Sure."

"To flatter you."

Hamilton laughed.

"Mr. Rossen's office. Miss Hannigan speaking."

"This is Megan Carter. Of the *Chronicle-News?*"

"Oh yes. Miss Carter. And what can we not do for you today?"

"I suppose you could not let me talk to Mr. Rossen."

"Easy. Mr. Rossen's in a meeting right now."

"Too bad."

"Any message?"

"Yeah. Say I want to know how he spells Gallagher. With one *f* or two."

"Hold on for a minute."

Click. Silence. Meg looked at Justice through the doors of the booth.

"Meg?" Rossen's voice sounded heartily amused. "What's all this about?"

"Gallagher."

"Is that supposed to blow me away? Who's Gallagher?"

"The guy who did Diaz."

"No shit. Jesus. Then you *really* better tell me who he is. Otherwise I'll get you for obstruction of justice." He laughed. She heard the click-click-click of his lighter. "Where'd you hear this baloney?"

"Sources, Elliot."

"Like who?"

"Uh uh. What's source for the goose isn't source for the gander. I don't reveal sources. Otherwise you wouldn't talk to me."

"Do I?"

"True," Meg agreed. "On the other hand, I'm going into print with this story, and—"

"You got enough to print?"

"Absolutely."

"Then you don't need to talk to me, right?"

"Neat."

"Come on, Megan. You know what the rule is. I can neither confirm nor deny nor comment on any investigation that may or may not be going on in this office. That's the rule. Okay?"

"Okay. All I need is five minutes of your time."

"Well, it's gonna be a dull five minutes."

"You're on. When?"

"Three o'clock."

"Terrific."

"It won't be."

She hung up the phone and then laughed. Not bad. She'd been playing with a lousy low pair of deuces and she'd just pulled a bluff that could take the whole pot.

Miss Hannigan eyed her with baleful surprise. Miss Hannigan was forty and excessively groomed. "You're early," she said.

"Guess again."

"He's late?" Frowning, Miss Hannigan looked at her watch. "He said if he was late, you should wait in his office." Miss Hannigan stood now and led the way in. "There's a coffeepot there. I guess help yourself."

"Why, thank you," Meg said, but Miss Hannigan was busily closing the door.

Meg looked around.

The office was large, neurotically neat, and furnished in a style that you'd have to call French, or at least that you'd have to call French's Mustard. On the windows were heavy, mustard-colored drapes that matched exactly the mustard of the walls, the wall-to-wall carpet, the three-cushion couch, and the visitor's wing chair at the side of the desk. The effect of this total immersion in mustard was, she imagined, to mentally prepare you to encounter a hot dog.

The hot dog was late.

An electric coffeepot burbled on a shelf. She half-filled a mug that said MUGSHOT on it, and settled into waiting in the wings of the chair, rehearsing how to handle the upcoming scene. Rossen undoubtedly would stick to his line ("I can neither confirm nor deny nor comment . . ."), so the problem was in getting him to move from the script. The problem was, how?

She glanced at his desk: a gold cigarette box, a plastic Snoopy, a piggy-bank that offered THE BUCK STOPS HERE. Lighting up a cigarette, she reached for an ashtray that said UP YOUR ASH! and then saw the file. It was right on the desk. In the middle of the desk. It was blue and the funny saying on its cover was GALLA-GHER.

Turning, she looked at the door.

The door was still closed. Miss Hannigan's Selectric clattered beyond with a rat-ta-tat, Katie-Gibbs-rhythm.

Okay.

7.

CONFIDENTIAL MEMO FOR: Elliot Rossen
               FROM: Robert M. Keener
            SUBJECT: Gallagher, Michael A.
             CASE #: 75-27

ENCLOSURES: Transcripts of 20 interviews; 31 August–
            2 September. Interviewing agents: Bloom-
            garten, Hamilton, Keener, McDermott.

Following is an edited transcript of a conversation between Agt. R. Keener and Nicole Peralta. Peralta is
Gallagher's secy/asst; age 37, attractive, divorced. Interview conducted (Friday) 31 August in Gallaher's warehouse.

PERALTA: If you're undercover, you blew it.
KEENER: Pardon?
PERALTA: You're fuzz. Who else'd walk around in a
navy blue suit? Sweet Jesus. It's gotta be ninety outside.
KEENER: Eighty.
PERALTA: You'd know. So what are you here for?
KEENER: I just want to ask you some questions. That's
all. About Michael Gallagher.
PERALTA: Show me your badge.
KEENER: Card.
PERALTA: Well, you're better-looking than your pic-
ture. Why?
KEENER: Just a lousy photographer.
PERALTA: Why do you want to ask questions, I mean.
KEENER: Routine investigation.
PERALTA: Oh, yeah. Well, I guess I know *that* routine.
The Routine routine. Whatever you guys think he did,
he didn't. I can tell you *that* much. Michael is clean.
KEENER: Uh-huh. And where is he now, do you know?
PERALTA: Gone fishing.
KEENER: Cute.

PERALTA: But true, *exigente*. They went on his boat. They'll be back on Tuesday.
KEENER: They?
PERALTA: Him and Johnny Ortega.
KEENER: Uh-huh. How long you been working here?
PERALTA: Me? I'd say about a year and a half.
KEENER: Uh-huh. Were you working here August the 10th?
PERALTA: If August the 10th was a weekday, yeah.
KEENER: Yes. Do you know where Gallagher was? On Friday afternoon, August the 10th.
PERALTA: Yeah. He was here.
KEENER: Would you look at his calendar?
PERALTA: No. I don't think so.
KEENER: Why not? You afraid he's got something to hide? I can pick up a warrant.

Keener insert: Peralta hesitates; opens a green leather notebook; the day is crossed out, a big pencilled X that covers the page. End insert.

KEENER: I see it. Do you happen to know where he was?
PERALTA: No. He told me it was personal business. That's all he said to me. I remember now, he crossed it out two days before.
KEENER: On the 8th?
PERALTA: And he still didn't do it.
KEENER: Do what?
PERALTA: Do whatever the hell you've been asking about.
KEENER: Uh-huh. Did he ever have trouble on the docks? I mean, with the dockers.
PERALTA: Never.
KEENER: Did you ever meet Joseph Diaz?
PERALTA: Me? No. Why would I? Oh! If you mean, was he ever in the office? No. He wasn't. And suddenly I don't think I like where you're going.
KEENER: And where do you think I'm going, Nicole?
PERALTA: Out! *Vamos*. The door's over there.

The following is an edited transcript of a conversation

between Agent R. Keener and Anthony Ross. 1 September. Ross, 57, a retired machinist from Camden, New Jersey, is Gallagher's neighbor at 127 Abingdon Place. Interview conducted in Ross's living room.

ROSS: Yeah, sure. I can tell you about him. But nothin' that's good. He brings down the neighborhood, you know what I mean? Got a whole buncha greasers there, goin' in and out.

KEENER: What's "greasers"?

ROSS: Greasers? *Greasers!* C'mon, you know what're greasers. Spics and spades.

KEENER: How about Sicilians?

ROSS: What the hell are *they?*

KEENER: Italians.

ROSS. Oh. Wouldn't know about that. You know, like they say, "Spics and spades can break our haids, but dagos never harm us." (laughs)

KEENER: Yeah. I'd like to show you some pictures, Mr. Ross. Have you ever seen any of these guys around here?

Keener insert: Subject shown photographs of Frank Cavaletti, Santos Malderone, Colin McKee, Franklin McKee, and Carmen Spungeilli, in that order. End insert.

ROSS: Well, they don't look like greasers to me. Except for the last one.

KEENER: The last one. Does that mean you've seen him around?

ROSS: Nah. I just mean he looks like a greaser.

KEENER: What about women? What kind of women does Gallagher see?

ROSS: Greasers. (laughs) Or you know, like my wife says, she calls 'em 'greasettes.'

KEENER: Uh, you mean, uh . . . blacks and Hispanics?

ROSS: Nah, I mean chippies. But one of 'em's spic. Redhead. I heard him callin' her Nicky. She stays with him a lot.

KEENER: And who are the others?

ROSS: I could give a description.

KEENER: Fine.

ROSS: Tits. They all got these really tre*men*dous tits.

KEENER: Uh-huh.

ROSS: I mean, they got ten-gallon jugs.

KEENER: Anything else you've noticed?

ROSS: Yeah. There's one of 'em not too attractive. Skinny. Nervous. Messy. Like she never washes her hair.

KEENER: Greasy?

ROSS: Now what do you mean there, a chippie? I wouldn't say chippie. Dope fiend, maybe. Something like that. One night she goes over there hysterical. Crying. I know about that one 'cause he meets her outside. And he says to her, "Listen, you gotta calm down. Did you bring any pills?" So she tells him she didn't, so then they went in. Dope fiend, I figure. Something like that. I'm tryin' to think of what else I could tell you. Excuse me. I better go answer the phone.

Keener insert: Interview ended. His dog, it seemed, had been killed by a truck.

Unedited transcript. Agent E. Hamilton and John Oretga. 1 September. Subject is Gallagher's warehouse foreman, a black Hispanic; wiry, small; age 37; convicted felon, Burglary 3rd; did 48 months at Ossining Prison; 1970–74. Interview conducted in

Meg turned quickly at the knock on the door and, replacing the file on the desk, said, "Yes?"

Miss Hannigan entered. "I'm really so terribly sorry, Miss Carter. Mr. Rossen won't be able to meet with you today."

"I see."

"He's delayed at a meeting."

"I see."

"But he did say to give you his profoundest regrets, and remind you that even had he talked with you today . . ."

"Yes?"

Miss Hannigan licked at a smile. "That he wouldn't have been able to confirm or deny or comment on any in-progress activity that is or is not . . ."

8.

The sun was setting; the sky over Biscayne Bay had turned red. Keener walked slowly to the end of the pier, to the dockmaster's office. The sign on the awning said Shoreham Marina. The sign on the door said Back in an Hour.

The door wasn't locked.

On the wall, behind a scuffed, leather-top desk, was a six-foot map of the Shoreham Marina. Pushpins skewered the bright-colored tags that showed whose boat was docked at which slip.

Gallagher's boat was at slip 41. The *Rum-Runner II*. Keener took his jacket off and loosened his tie.

It was a long walk.

The bay seemed to be on fire in the light. On the decks of the bigger, flashier yachts, the sunburned beauties, dressed in their whites, were sipping their frosty piña coladas and laughing their frosty, white little laughs. Music drifted, aimless, on the air.

The neighborhood, just like the sun, went down. Every marina had neighborhoods, he knew. From the cruisers, powerboats, sailboats, charterboats, down to the slums where the eighth-hand twenty-foot Chris Crafts live. Slip 41 was at the end of Park Avenue, right where the neighborhood started to slide—from million-dollar yachts down to two hundred grand.

Forty one was empty; he'd expected it to be.

The man on the *Katie* at slip 42 looked up and said, "You lookin fer Gallagher?"

"Yeah."

He squinted at Keener. He was holding a gummy-looking rag in his hand and working at the big brass rail on the stern. He looked about sixty; rangy and brown; sun-faded jeans and a grime-colored shirt. "Gone," he said. "Back on Tuesday. Tomorra."

"Gone all weekend?"

"Yep."

"Too bad."

"Well . . . not fer him."

Keener shifted his weight. "Missed him last week when I was over here, too."

"Yeah? When was that?"

"Week ago, maybe."

"Funny." The old man polished more brass. "He's been over here most every night since the fire."

"The fire?"

"Must've been toward the end of July. Looked like the Fourth. Fireworks, you know?"

"What happened?"

"Gutted the galley, that's what. Took him till now just to get her fixed up. Been workin like a dog."

"What started the fire?"

The old man put down his rag and looked thoughtful. "You one of them insurance adjustors, or what?"

"Worse," Keener said.

"Hell, nothin worse than an insurance adjustor."

"Fed?" Keener tried.

"Maybe." The old man laughed. "Maybe so. Hard to tell these days. You fellas goin in and out of fashion so fast. I suppose you got good ones and bad ones, though." He squinted. "Want a beer?"

"Yeah," Keener said. "No. I mean, I'm still on duty. Got a Coke?"

"I guess."

There was a gangplank rigged to the deck. When Keener was on board, the old man studied him with weathered blue eyes and then held out a big, brown, knuckly hand. "Name's Charlie Wilson, and you're . . . ?"

"Bob Keener."

"Yeah?" Wilson cocked his head. "Rings a bell."

"Don't know why it should."

"Beats hell outta me." Wilson walked off. He came back with some fairly cold bottles from below and settled in a captain's chair opposite Keener, lit a cigarette, and then watched him in silence.

Finally, Keener said, "Made up your mind?"

"Yep. You're a good-enough one," Wilson said. "What's your question?"

"The fire. Were you here when it happened?"

"Sure. Always here. I live here. Got a nice little deck down below. If you mean did I see any funny business, no. I was sleepin. Woke up with the goddam bang. Thing blew a big, mean hole in his deck, and that's a real good mahogany he's got in there, too. Lucky I was here."

"What blew a hole?"

"Well, that's the question. Now, you figure it's the propane tank in his stove. Only then you gotta figure the tank's near to empty. Otherwise, you figure it'd blow up the pier."

"Is that what the fire marshal said?"

"Oh, yeah. Question is, how come she acted like that?"

"Got any answers?"

"Nope, not a one. Got any more questions?"

Keener lit a cigarette. Tossing the match to the water below, he hooked his leg around the arm of the chair. "What kind of work did you do, Charlie? Before you retired."

"Me? Had a dairy farm. Colorado. Front range of the Rockies. That's land there, you know. That is goddam . . . land." He shook his head slowly, then shrugged. "So of course, like it happens, the developers came. I had three hundred acres. They were movin all around me. Startin to feel like a chess game, you know? They were puttin me in check. I suppose you don't want to have a nice long talk about soil erosion, but the point is, I'm gettin flooded on the one hand and drought on the other. So hell, I just figured better sell it while I could. So I bought *Miss Katie* here and maybe I'll just up and sail around the world. Had it with the land. Try the sea." He sniffed, ran a big-boned hand on his jaw. "Why'd you want to know that?"

"Just to know who I'm talking to."

"Well . . . if you find that out, let me know."

"Bull," Keener said. "You know Gallagher well?"

"What you mean by bull?"

"I mean you know goddam well who you are. How well you know Gallagher?"

Wilson shook his head, grinning. "I guess not as well as all that. Better since the fire. I helped put it out, so he buys me a new engine. You imagine that? Buys me an engine. What a thing."

"So you like him."

"Oh, hell. Not just for that."

"For what then?"

"For reasons people like people. Listen, he's a likable fella, that's all. And I don't mean he's one of them smiley types, either. Loner, I'd say."

"Doesn't have much company?"

"Used to. Not so much any more. When he first come down, there was girls all the time. Different ones, only they was always the same. Cookies from the same little cookie-cutter. Blondes. You know the ones. Easier to make than a bad cup of coffee. Anyway, he all of a sudden just stops. So now he comes mostly to the boat by himself. Or that black guy he works with. Sometimes a redhead but not very much. I don't think she likes the water."

"Uh-huh. Ever see him with a messy-looking girl? Nervous type?"

"Well . . . I wouldn't call her messy. Pretty thing. Skinny. But nervous, I'd say. He's off with her now, this weekend."

"Alone?"

"Well she didn't bring her mother."

"Uh-huh. Know her name?"

"Nope. She's a dark-haired girl. Kinda tall. Kinda pale. Is that the girl you're lookin for?"

"Who says I'm lookin for a girl?" Keener said.

Charlie Wilson squinted in the darkening light. "Ask me, you look like a fella that needs one. Want another Coke there?"

9.

McAdam was reading the copy as she typed. He was making her nervous.

" 'Under investigation'?" he sneered. "Weak. Can't we call him a suspect?"

"Sure." She looked up. "But we still don't know what he's suspected of."

"Suspected *in*. That's a nice little weasel. 'Suspected *in* the murder of Diaz.' "

"Gee, and I thought you were a city editor."

"What's that supposed to mean?"

"It means only a coroner can pronounce a man dead, and even a coroner has to have a body. No body, remember?"

"Quibbler. Okay. 'Presumed murder,' then. Believe me, you're missing for a month and you're dead."

"They're not even sure Judge Crater is dead. And what about Bonnano?"

McAdam looked at her.

"Joseph Bonnano. In 1964, he's subpoenaed as a witness in a grand jury probe. Only, on the way, as he's driving to the court, he's supposedly kidnapped by seven armed men. Two years later, he shows up alive, and entirely well, except he's afflicted with a permanent smile." She answered McAdam's glare with a shrug.

"Even Keener," he said, "presumed he was dead. And how about 'prime'? He's a 'prime suspect.' "

Meg shook her head. "I don't know if he's prime. Maybe they've got someone prime-er."

" 'Key.' The key suspect."

"*A* key suspect."

"Christ," McAdam spluttered. "Whose side are you on? You want anyone to *read* this story, or what? You keep watering it down." He paused, lit a cigarette. "All right. Let's decide about attribution."

" 'Informed sources.' 'Well-informed sources.' 'Highly

placed—.' Why did he give it to me, Mac? He leaves me in a room with 'Michael Gallagher' written on the walls, and then he won't see me? What's his angle in that?"

"Maybe he didn't know the file was there?"

"You believe that?"

"No." McAdam blew smoke. "On the other hand, I now believe in Santa Claus. 'Sources close to the investigation.' "

"Knowledgeable sources."

"Knowledgeable sources."

"Answer my question. Why did he leak?"

"I don't know why. Because Keener just told us they were up against walls. Because maybe he wanted to contradict Keener. Because maybe he wanted to one-up Quinn. Because maybe he wanted to get into your pants. How the hell do *I* know? Christ! If we stop to figure why people leak, we'd be publishing monthly. When you finish that, take it in to Cardigan."

"Fine. But I want to get Gallagher first."

"Honey, you got 'im." McAdam raised his middle finger in the air, grinning.

"I meant on the phone. For comment?"

"Hey. No way. You put it off till five or six minutes to presstime. Then if you can't reach him, you've tried, and you add, 'He was unavailable for comment.' "

"Wow. Is that fair?"

"Grow up," McAdam said.

Keener kicked his shoes off and walked to the stove. "Want some coffee?"

"I guess so." Hamilton shrugged. "No. Not really."

"Don't worry. It's not really coffee," Keener said. "It's instant. It tastes like your bathtub water." He filled up a cup and then looked at it balefully. "Shit. I bet they used this in black-powder guns." He moved to the living room. "So what did you want to talk to me about?"

"Well—"

"You want to sit on the couch or the chair?"

"Shit, I don't care, man."

"Good. Take the chair. I want to lie on the couch."

Hamilton sat. He looked around briefly. "Jesus. This place is depressing, you know?"

"I know." Keener took in a belt of his coffee.

"So why don't you buy some furniture or something?"

"If I furnished it, I might think I lived here. Go on."

"I want to talk about Gallagher."

"Fine. Go on."

"I think you're wrong about him, Keener. I think he looks good."

"You mean you think he looks bad. You think *I* think he's good, and you think he's bad. Is that what you mean?"

"Yeah."

"Go on."

"Isn't that what you think?"

"Doesn't matter what I think. Go on."

"I think he's lookin good as whodunit, okay? So I just want to tell you what I learned."

"Did you tell it to Rossen?"

"No. Why would I? I'm telling it to you. Right?"

"Go on."

"Okay. He bought a gun. Forget about parole violations, dig the date. August the seventh."

"Where did he buy it?"

"From a badguy. A good gun. A thirty-eight with a nose job. A Colt."

"Go on."

"I spoke to a guy named Javinsky at the Shoreham Marina. Apparently the fire was put out by the staff. Javinsky's a night guard and he's also an ex–arson squad cop and he said he thinks somebody turned on the stove and blew out the flame. Or *might* have, he said."

"So it *might* have been an accident."

"So it *might* have been on purpose."

"Name two."

"It might have been a message from the mob: play ball. Do Diaz. Or the other way around. Diaz had some pretty rough soldier boys too. So maybe that was Gallagher's motive: revenge. I don't know. The fire was July twenty-ninth. Thirteen days before D-day."

"Is thirteen significant?"

"Cut it out, Keener. What's significant is Gallagher never reported it. Didn't even claim his insurance on it."

"Oh." Keener squinted. "Which leads you to assume . . . ?"

"That he knew damn well that it wasn't an accident. That he didn't want it closely investigated."

"Yeah. Go on."

"That, and then where the hell was he on the tenth."

"Right." Keener nodded.

"So what do you think?"

"I think we better find out."

"That's what I thought. I mean, I think it looks good— Doesn't it?"

"Christ." Keener laughed. "Ask me again when you've lived a little longer. You want to have dinner?"

"Can't. Got a date. What's wrong with it?"

"Dates?" Keener looked at him. "Nothing."

"Forget it. How're you comin on with Saigon Sue?"

"Meg?" Keener laughed. "She hasn't gotten any more military secrets."

"She's a bitch, man. Watch her."

"I know what to watch."

"Yeah, she's watchable. I'll sure give her that. An eleven."

"Maybe you're the one that better watch out."

"I could take her or leave her."

"And she's really not a bitch. She's just . . ."

"She's just what?"

"Young."

"Yeah? She'll grow into it, then. She's sharp and ambitious."

Keener looked up. "So are you, ole buddy."

"That's different."

Keener laughed.

Hamilton shrugged, and then laughed at himself.

Meg watched Cardigan reading the copy. Lawyers went over words slowly, she thought. As though they were going over minefields. Christ. He looked up, nodded, and impaled her with his sharp, pouchy gray eyes. There was something decidedly Dickensian about him. She could picture him rapping on the knuckles of scribes; conversely, she could not see him blessing Tiny Tim. "Imposing" was the word for Josiah Cardigan; he imposed suppositions that taxed your wit.

"*So*, Miss Carter." His tone was sarcastic; he enunciated clearly, laying italics on a lot of his words. "*So*. You've written us a *story*, I see."

She nodded.

"Odd," he said. "Odd. The appellation of 'story.' 'Story' rather smacks of fiction, don't you think?"

She was silent; then she said, "This one isn't fiction."

"Ah!" He nodded. "But of course!" He nodded. "But of course I imagine that's what everybody says. Including that rather imaginative person on the *Washington Post*." He nodded again. "And including that young fellow up in Toronto who got his paper sued for over two million dollars. Granted—Canadian dollars. But still . . ."

Meg said nothing; she waited.

"Let's suppose . . ." he swiveled in his chair, "let's suppose for a moment we are Mr. Michael Gallagher. As such, we might feel understandably miffed. We might feel the sting of being labeled a murderer."

"We didn't say—"

"Oh come come *come* now, Miss Carter! That is clearly the implication, is it not? Even though the words are most cunningly chosen. And surely Mr. Gallagher, a, uh"—he frowned at the manuscript—"a 'key suspect' in a, uh, 'presumed murder'?—surely Mr. Gallagher will ferret this out. And so will his colleagues, neighbors, and friends." Cardigan paused. "So now let's suppose, just for argument's sake, that he is neither a killer, *nor*, Miss Carter, the subject of a full investigation for same. And then further—"

"But he is. I saw it. The file. And believe me, they're investigating—"

"*Madam!*" Cardigan exhaled his impatience. "My concern here is not with the truth, but the *law*. I have not been employed by this great publication for the noble endeavor of protecting the truth, but rather to protect, if you will, our ass." He let the word linger on the air for a moment, then leaned back slowly and nodded. "All right. Let's accept your allegation for the moment as truth: you've indeed seen the file. But where is our assurance that the *file* is the truth? What is Truth, Miss Carter?"

"Oh, Christ."

"Quite possibly, but Biblical truth has been subject to debate. However, we will grant you that the file and its contents, ostensibly, as of this moment, seem true. Are we clear? Are we *legally* clear, Miss Carter?"

"We should be."

"Ah! Should! And the sick should be well and the virtuous triumph. And what if the contents turn out to be false?"

"I don't know."

"It then becomes a question of malice: was it present or absent in reporting this lie?"

"Hey look, sir, I don't even know Michael Gallagher. I never even *heard* of him till Friday afternoon. So why would I want to be malicious about him?"

"Lovely. Let's confine ourselves to legal malice, shall we? As defined in the case of the *Times* versus Sullivan. The import of the case was that newspapers needn't prove the truth of what they print, but merely that our fictions have been framed without malice, *if*, that is, the person being libeled is, among other things, a public figure." Cardigan rattled his pen on the desk. "Query: has Gallagher ever been discussed in a public procedings? Some legislative body that was sniffing out crime?"

"I don't know."

"Ah, yes. Ignorance remains a most charming defense. Has he ever been arrested? Convicted?"

"Yes. For assaulting an officer."

"Splendid. Did he do it quite publicly?"

"Yes. I read there were two hundred people at—"

"Magnificent! Query: is the criminally convicted son of a criminal public figure thereby a public figure himself?"

"Yes?"

"I'm afraid it's quite doubtful. Query further: is the criminally convicted son of a criminal public figure who is now involved in a criminal investigation of great public interest *thereby* a public figure?"

"No?"

"Perhaps. I'd say he has a tinge of public figure about him, but I'd feel a lot better were he, say, Robert Redford." Cardigan was silent, musing for a moment.

"Is that a yes or a no?" Meg tried. "Can we print it?"

"Patience, Miss Carter. We still have another few hurdles to go. According to the case of *Gertz* v. *Welch*, even if our subject cannot be considered as a public figure, and even if our story is false on its face, he cannot sue and win unless he can prove we were negligent. Were we?"

"Was *I*? I don't think so. No."

"Is there anything further you could reasonably do to ascertain the truth of the story you propose?"

Meg shook her head.

"Have you spoken to him?"

"No. Not yet. But I plan to."

"Good. Should he talk, you will please to include his impassioned denials, which will help create the general illusion of fairness. Should he not, we can hardly be responsible for errors he refuses to correct. If we try, but don't reach him, at least we'll have tried, and the judge will appreciate our effort."

Meg nodded. "Are you telling me to print?"

"I'm telling you, madam, that the vaunted truth of your story is irrelevant. We are absent of knowledge that the story is false, therefore we are also absent of malice. We have done our very best and therefore we have not been negligent. So! We may therefore defame the man any way we like and he is powerless to harm us. Democracy is served."

"We can print?"

"Roll the presses, as we once used to say."

10.

Gallagher woke to the plink of the rain. He opened his eyes and squinted at the hard, gray sea and the sky. He moved in the deck chair. His body felt stiff. Yawning, he stood, tucking his shirt tail firmly in his jeans, and then stretched, widely, and his shirt popped out. The rain was getting heavier. He went down below. In the cabin, Teresa was asleep on the bed, with the overheads on and the radio playing. Afraid of the dark, afraid of the quiet. Christ, poor baby, Gallagher thought.

He moved to the galley, deciding he wouldn't try to grind any coffee since the noise might wake her, and opened up a can of Jamaican espresso. He carefully measured some into the pot.

The radio announced it was seventy degrees at 10:47, and would probably rain. He thought about tossing the radio topside and seeing if it learned from experience. The rain was really battering now. Through the porthole, he could see Charlie Wilson next door, pacing in his cabin. Gallagher waved.

Lighting the burner, he squinted at the brand new Safetysure stove, giving it the warning finger, "Be good," and quietly moved himself into the head.

The radio reported that traffic was lousy, as though that were news.

He looked at his beard. The last time he'd shaved was on Friday morning, and already his face had a goddam lawn. It had snowed on the lawn. White was frosted all over the thing, and he wondered why the hair on his head was still dark. Or else why the hair in his beard should be white. Forty-seven. Was that so old? He decided not to wait for the answer, and shaved.

Terry'd left her comb on the side of the sink. He ran it through his hair and thought about her, what he could do for her. Nothing, he decided. Nothing but be there when she needed him; that, and maybe sometimes get her to relax, cart her off for weekends, and lay her in the sun. Lie her in the sun. He did not want to lay her. And anyway, sex was the last thing she needed. Dr. Gallagher's Magical Medical Cure (and Packaged Singles Weekend for Two) had included a few complementary cocktails, some freshwater fishing, some sun, and some food.

Food. He'd better fix her a nice big breakfast and make sure she ate it before he took off.

Quietly, he opened the door of the head.

The radio coughed up a Major Breakthrough in the Diaz Case.

Gallagher reached for a carton of eggs.

A Mobster's Son was a Primary Suspect.

He reached for a bowl.

The Primary Suspect was Michael Gallagher.

He turned, and saw Terry standing at the door.

Quinn picked up the phone and dialed so fast he got a lousy recording. "The number you have dialed is not in operation. Please be sure the number—"

He tried it again.

A kid said, "H'lo?"

"Is your father there?"

"Yeah. My daddy's in the toilet."

"Exactly," Quinn said.

"You want me to get 'im?"

"Yeah. Tell him Harrison Quinn's on the phone."

"Okay," the kid said, and then it sounded like the telephone had fallen downstairs.

Quinn plucked a spoon from the dining room table. His wife poured him coffee and he waved her away angrily. She answered with a look of reproach (the lifted-up brows and the thrust-out mouth) and retreated to the kitchen, a thousand bucks of lingerie clinging to her rump. A nice little rump, he was forced to admit, and Melanie really liked to twitch it around—almost anyplace except between the Porthault sheets. She'd bought herself a husband, Quinn was aware, for the same kind of reason that she bought those sheets: she wanted something classy to dress up her bed, and in terms of all the labor involved in the upkeep, well, what the hell, let the maid do it. Still, in all fairness, it was hard to complain. He was getting her money's worth.

Rossen came on. "What's up?" he said briskly.

"That's what *I'd* like to know. I read in the papers we're investigating Gallagher."

"We?"

"Yeah, we," Quinn said. "The Justice Department, remember?"

"Sure. Where you worked before you went into politics."

"You don't have to work to rile me, Elliot. You've already done it. I want to know what the hell you're doing with Gallagher."

"Investigating, Harrison. Just like it says."

"And that's another question. *Why* does it say? You been leaking to Carter?"

"Me? Christ, no."

"Then how'd she find out?"

"Hell, I dunno. But my personal bet would be Bigmouth Keener. He's screwing her. That, or the other way around. Anyway, he's blabbered before, and you know it."

Quinn gave it thought and then nodded. "I guess."

"On the other hand, I'm not exactly sorry he did."

"*What?*"

"Never mind."

"Never *mind?*" Quinn said. "Sweet God. You got the balls now to tell me never *mind?* I *mind*, Elliot. I mind when some stupid little newspaper twitch gets the news before I do. Now share it. Fast. I want to know what the hell you're doing with Gallagher."

"Investigating."

"What."

"Whatever."

"Whatever. That's nice. That means you've got absolutely nothing on him."

"Yet."

"So what're you looking for?"

"Something. I don't know."

In the background, Quinn heard the kid start to wail and a woman's voice yelling bloody murder at the kid.

"Christ," Rossen said, "he's Malderone's nephew. His

father sold booze to every hood on the coast. He knows those guys. And he either knows something or he knows how to learn it."

"So you're squeezing him."

"So?"

"It's a cheap shot, Elliot. Harassment's cheap. If you want to find out what he knows, then talk to him. Talk to him directly."

"Not yet," Rossen said. "Not till he knows we got a trump in our hand. Otherwise he'll tell us to fuck ourselves."

"Fine. I believe you know how."

"Funny. And then what? After all that."

"Then, if you think you've got a reason, investigate. Quietly. But no surveillance and no harassment. And not unless you've got a better reason than now. If you've got a case, make it. If you don't, back off."

Rossen guffawed. "What's the matter there, Harrison? You lookin for the ACLU endorsement? Don't worry. You don't need it. If we wrap this baby, you're in like Quinn."

"And if we don't, you're out."

"You can't fire me, Harry. So don't get grand."

"I can warn you, Elliot. It's my district, and I won't have you running wild in it, hear? If you want to be a cowboy, go back to New York."

"Swell. And I'll tell you where you can go, too."

In the background, the kid started yammering again. The woman was shrilling, and Quinn heard the definite sound of a slap. The kid wailed harder.

"Aw, shit," Rossen said. "Hey, look, Joey Diaz was a decent little guy. And some creeps knocked him over and we haven't got zip. And it's not only that. You got a grand jury sitting on waterfront crime? Your grand jury might as well sit on their *ears* for all they're gonna hear. So we gotta do something about it, okay?"

"Why Gallagher?"

"Why not?"

"Because he's probably clean."

"And so what if he is? Hey, look, I'm not trying to *convict* the man, dig? I just want to get him to play a little ball."

"Or else."

"What the hell. If he's really such an honest, upstanding citizen, he'll *want* to play ball."

"And if tries to, they'll kill him."

"So? What the hell. Then we'll get 'em for *that.*"

Quinn was silent; then he said slowly, "Not funny, Elliot."

"Who's being funny?"

"Is that what you're up to?"

"No. Of course not."

"Say it with conviction."

"No. Of course not. And anyway, Harry, why the hell would you care. I mean, you want to get elected now, don't you?"

Harrison Quinn took a breath. "Not over someone's dead body," he said.

"Yeah?" Rossen laughed. "Say it with conviction."

11.

The first edition of the *Times-Gazette* did not have the story.

Ha! Meg thought.

On the other hand, the final edition had an item—a four-inch box at the foot of page 1—informing the public that the Justice Department, in the persons of both Mssrs. Rossen and Quinn, absolutely would not confirm published reports of a full investigation of Michael Gallagher. The way it was worded, the refusal to confirm had been twisted to appear like a flat denial. It was practically awesome. And anyone who didn't think writing was a skill, Meg considered, should be forced to examine how the structure of a sentence, the seemingly casual use of a verb, or even the exact position of a comma, could alter the interpretation of a thought. Her story had been skillfully dismantled by pros, and you couldn't put your finger on exactly how they'd done it. Unless you knew exactly how to do it yourself.

And dammit, she thought, as she drove down the Harborway, how could they give her this gratuitous zap? Even though they hadn't really mentioned her name, they'd attacked her integrity. Page-one box. The bastards, she thought. She turned onto Flagler and stopped at the light. The rain hammered down. Even the sky was stealing her thunder.

She arrived at the newsroom in a terrible mood.

"Hail," McAdam said. "Our Reporter of the Year. What's the matter, kid? You oughtta be grinning ear to ear. We beat the *Times-Gazette* and they're sulking. That's good. Even Edwards called in from his vacation paradise."

"And?"

"For a change he's happy, okay? Get happy yourself. That was damn good reporting. The Nancy Drew–Brenda Starr Memorial Award. Which is better than a Pulitzer,

from what I've been hearing. The prize is a free cup of
coffee. Help yourself."

Meg poured some coffee from the pot on the table that
percolated twenty-four hours a day and was otherwise
dubbed The Eternal Light. It tasted like Eternal Darkness.

"Was it really?"

McAdam squinted. "Was what really what?"

"Was it really good reporting?"

"Oh, Jesus. Women." McAdam walked off, then
turned. "And stay with it. See what you can get on Gallagher. Background. Foreground. Underground. Get it.
See if you can talk to him."

"I'm not exactly sure he'll be—" Meg stopped cold.
The man in the doorway, who was talking to Alicia, who
was pointing at Meg, was handsome and tall. He was
rangy and tan. He was dark-haired, blue-eyed, and dread-
fully mad. He was madder than hell. He was Michael
Gallagher.

She moved to her desk and developed an intense interest in a pencil. She couldn't take her eyes off it. Ticon-
deroga #2, it said. Medium. Something rather large and
beige was approaching. Gallagher was wearing a trenchcoat; beige. Or maybe it was only the Sahara Desert,
which was rumored to be shifting at the annual rate of
a—

"You're Megan Carter." He said it in a tone that could
also be used to say, "You're Lizzie Borden." His eyes
were an icy, merciless blue. "Where the hell did you get
this?" The paper was slammed on her desk with a *whack*.
His getting-out-of-jail picture glared from the page. He
glared much better in person, she thought. It was chilling;
those eyes under straight black brows. She could believe
he was a killer.

"I . . . um," she said, but nothing seemed to follow.
"I . . . uh," she tried again, upending the coffee cup and
watching as the coffee started pooling on her dress. It was
making an absolutely fascinating stain, "I, uh . . . what
did you say?"

"I said where'd you get the story."

"Oh." The coffee was sliding down her leg; it was dripping on her shoe. She looked at the shoe and then glanced

up at Gallagher. "Look: either shoot me or help me, okay?"

"Is that a serious choice?" His eyes hadn't changed. He fumbled in the inside pocket of his coat, and for a very long second, she wondered if a Colt .22 would come out.

He tossed her a handkerchief; she started to use it. "So, uh, what can I do for you, Mr. Gallagher?"

"Answer my question."

"I can't."

"What the hell kind of answer is that?"

She looked at him quickly; his face was still hard: granite. "It's the truth," she told him. "I can't."

"Who can?"

"I, uh . . ."

McAdam moved in smoothly, announcing his name and his title. "What's the problem?" he said.

"I want to know the source of this story."

"I'm sorry."

"And you damn well ought to be. Repeat: I want to know the source of—"

"I'm sorry, but I can't tell you that."

"Swell. Terrific. You can tell half the world I'm a goddam *killer*, but you can't—"

"Now we didn't say that, Mr. Gallagher." Meg cleared her throat. "What we said was 'suspected.' "

"Suspected is the same thing as guilty."

"No it isn't."

"It isn't? Swell. Then how'd you like to live next door to the guy who's *suspected* of being Jack the Ripper?"

Meg said nothing.

"I think I have a right to confront my accuser. Who is it accused me?"

"No one," Meg said, "exactly . . . accused you."

"What we said," McAdam said, "is simply that you're being investigated."

"Swell. And how do you know that? I don't know that. How do you know that?"

"We're going in circles," McAdam said flatly. "Look. Last time. I'm sorry, but we never give out that information. If you want to know exactly what the government is doing, you'd better ask the government."

"I tried that. They don't give out that information."

She watched him: a statue in stone-cold fury. Controlled fury. Impacted rage. She hoped she'd remember that: "impacted rage." If she got another chance to write a story about him . . .

"Well, too bad," McAdam said. "Tough. Still—if you aren't connected with Diaz, what do you suppose they're lookin at you for?"

"They want to know when I stopped beating my wife. What the hell kind of ass-headed question is *that?*"

"Were you?" Meg said. "I mean, connected with—"

"No!"

"Can you prove you're not connected?"

"Lady, *I* don't have to prove a fuckin *thing!*"

"Did you ever meet Diaz?"

He opened his mouth, then closed it; he looked from McAdam to Meg. "So how come you didn't ask me that question before you started making up headlines about me?"

"I called, but there wasn't any answer."

"You should've called back."

"I had a deadline."

"Oh. Yeah. A deadline," he said.

McAdam cleared his throat. "This isn't productive. So unless there's something else we can do for you—"

"There is. Stop writing about me. And when all this is over—if it's really going on—you can do another headline, on how I'm not involved. I mean, look, what the hell, that's a big story too. 'Mobster's Son Is Disgustingly Clean.' Think about it. Jesus and Mary," he said. "Protecting your sources. You put me in a noose and you're protecting the hangman. Only it's a lynch mob. Terrific." He turned, shaking his head. "Ter*rif*ic," he muttered, and walked out the door.

It had stopped raining. The rain hadn't done much to lighten the air. It was hot and dull as a gray flannel suit. Gallagher tossed his coat to the carseat and rolled down the windows. He lit a cigarette and then smoked it, idly, looking in the rear-view mirror. Yeah. The silver Buick was still there behind him, two cars behind him and parked at the curb, with the two guys sitting in it: sunglasses, caps. He'd spotted them earlier on Biscayne Boul-

evard and once before that at the Shoreham. Tail.
Obvious tail. The only question that remained now was
who, the goons or the feds? And the question of whether
he could lose them.

He stubbed out his cigarette and started the motor.
They pulled out after him, keeping a distance of two or
three cars, and tailed him down Flagler. It occurred to
him that it didn't matter if he lost them. Whoever they
were, they could find him again, at the house, the warehouse, the boat. They'd kill him if they wanted to kill
him. If the guys were just browsing, they'd continue to
browse. What bothered him was being hung for a goat.
Always. Christ. Fourteen months for a punch on the jaw.
Guys could steal millions and do the same time. You
could kill an old lady and be out in a year. He lit another
cigarette. Jesus. In jail they'd all thought he was a bigshot. So guys'd come over and they'd ask him for smack.
So he'd smacked one—another of the world-famous
rights-to-the-jaw. The guy lost a tooth; the guard looked
away. Bigshot.

He watched them in the mirror again. Maybe he'd take
them for a sightseeing tour. Maybe they could use a vacation. Miami. It hadn't exactly been a day at the beach.
So maybe he just should have stayed in New York. Maybe.
And then again, probably not. Deny thy father and refuse thy name: Shakespeare. Terry. And the Repertory
Theater on Sheridan Square. He'd been thirty and drift-
ing; she'd been fresh, seventeen. And then she got involved with Geraldo, and acid, and lost her virginity to
four hundred guys on a weekend in the Hamptons. Or
two dozen guys. What difference did it make? But that's
the way he'd found her: in the East Hampton station,
waiting for a local, scudded and scared. And he'd scraped
her off the floor. She was twenty by then. He was already
married, respectable; he wasn't an actor anymore—unless
marriage was the phoniest act of them all. But anyway,
they'd both made the headlines with that one. MOBSTER'S
SON AND PALM BEACH HEIRESS (he'd taken her back to
his apartment to rest; he'd called a doctor; his wife had
been there) IN LURID LOVE NEST. Jesus. A plague on both
your houses.

The sun was coming out. The palm trees, shiny from

the downpour, glimmered. The glassy hotel fronts blinked in the light, and he stepped on the pedal for the sheer fucking hell of it. MOBSTER'S NEPHEW BUSTED FOR SPEED. The air felt good. He was going ninety. The road was still slick. GALLAGHER CRASHES IN GETAWAY CAR. He was topping a hundred. He knew where to turn. There were sirens now, vaguely in the distance. He turned. The Buick tried to follow him, couldn't. It missed; went into a boulder. Its hood was a mess. In the mirror he watched the two guys getting out. He eased off the pedal; he shrugged and then laughed.

HOOD CREAMS HOOD.

The day got worse.

12.

The following is an edited transcript of a conversation between Agts. R. Keener/E. Hamilton and Michael Gallagher. Interview conducted (Tuesday) 4 September in Gallagher's warehouse office.

GALLAGHER: Well, if it isn't old glassjaw.
KEENER: Yep.
GALLAGHER: If I deck you again, I guess they give me the chair.
KEENER: Probably.
GALLAGHER: You talked to Nicky and John. So I figure you're really investigating.
KEENER: Hell. We just happened to be in the neighborhood.
GALLAGHER: Cute.
HAMILTON: We were hoping you could straighten this out.
GALLAGHER: *You* were hoping.
KEENER: Can you tell us where you were on August the 10th?
GALLAGHER: Nope.
HAMILTON: Can you tell us why you purchased a gun?
GALLAGHER: What gun?
KEENER: It would help if you cooperated.
GALLAGHER: Yeah? Help who?
KEENER: You, maybe.
GALLAGHER: (laughs) Only maybe. That's nice. Jesus. You guys really think I did Diaz?
KEENER: Jesus. I don't think at all. No brains. I'm a rock-dumb Fed. You know that.
GALLAGHER: Yeah.
KEENER: Is there anything else you might happen to know? Something that could help us?
GALLAGHER: No.

KEENER: If you do, we came here to offer you special arrangements.
GALLAGHER: (laughs) Like protection?
HAMILTON: Yeah. That's right.
GALLAGHER: Sure you will. Me and Reagan and the pope. What else've you got? Another identity? Another city?
KEENER: If you like.
GALLAGHER: I don't. I like my own name and I like my address. And I don't know *nada*. So why don't you call off your dumb fuckin tail?
KEENER: What tail?
GALLAGHER: Right.
KEENER: You aren't being tailed.
GALLAGIIER: Right. Forget it.
KEENER: Who's tailing you?
GALLAGHER: Forget it. No one.
KEENER: You want some protection?
GALLAGHER: From who? From no one?
KEENER: Call me if you need any help.
GALLAGHER: Keener?
KEENER: Yeah?
GALLAGHER: Hold your breath till I call.

Keener put the typed report in an envelope, along with some other reports about Gallagher, and shoved it in a drawer. He wasn't exactly sure what he was doing, withholding the information from Rossen, but then he wasn't sure what Rossen was doing. Every report on Gallagher was clean, or relatively clean, or at least up till now, which either meant Gallagher was relatively clean—or dirty and smart.

True, there were the questions of the fire and the gun, and Hamilton's reasoning wasn't absurd. Or no more absurd than life often was. So let Hamilton work it and see what he found. Keener could imagine some other connections that were totally unrelated to Diaz, but whatever the reason the gun was still there—a parole violation—and Rossen could be cute enough to prosecute that. Or jump it. If the race wasn't always to the swift, then it was, Rossen figured, to the gun-jumper. So.

Keener pulled a key out and locked up the drawer.

*　　*　　*

The *Times-Gazette* had continued to sulk. Their Wednesday editorial, entitled "On the Pressing Problems of the Press," inveighed against the use of unattributed sources, especially in stories with no other source. "The possible motives of informants," it said, "must always be carefully, cautiously weighed, and then balanced with other documentary proof, or at least with convincingly supportive evidence. While, clearly, the use of such confidential sources is helpful—indeed, often vital—to the press, a reporter should never make use of them lightly, even though their purpose may be to shed light on the shadowy corners of corruption and crime."

Meg read that one over coffee and toast and choked on it. Maybe it was only the toast, but it felt like a large and grim editorial was stuck in her craw. But nothing, she told herself, not even newsprint, was that black and white. She *had* seen the documentary proof; she just couldn't say so. Rossen had leaked because he couldn't speak openly, or not without putting his ass on the line. Most people talked off the record out of fear, for their jobs or their lives, and they had to be protected. ("You're protecting the hangman," Gallagher had said.)

It was awesomely hot and muggy outside. Indian summer. Warpath weather. In the Federal Building, the reception was cool. She arrived for her ten o'clock meeting with Quinn to learn that "he does not wish to speak to you." Nice. Nothing remotely indirect about that. No little white lies about being called away, just a flat-out "does not wish to speak to you." Swell.

And neither, apparently, did anyone else. Reagan, of the DEA, was "out to lunch" (at a quarter of eleven) and Bolt, of the IRS, was "in China."

Meg was in coventry and wasn't sure why.

Only the court clerk, Marlin, was friendly, offering the subjects of the morning's proceedings.

"Yup. We got earth-shakin news around here. Motion to sever, set aside verdict, and three postponements. That's it. Take yer pick."

"That's all?"

"How it goes."

"Yeah. How it goes."

* * *

Meg said, "Good morning."

Donna said, "I don't believe it."

"You're right. It's a lousy morning."

"Yeah. That too."

"What else?"

"I don't *believe* you're coming into this office."

"Oh."

"I don't *believe* you're gonna make it out alive. And, I tell you, after yesterday—"

"What happened yesterday?"

"Your story hit the paper and the shit hit the fan. Which blew it on me."

"I don't get it. Why you?"

"Why me? I'd told Keener you were in here on Friday. Remember? Doesn't matter. Keener remembers, and I think he suspects me."

"Of being my source?"

"Of something. I couldn't tell what he suspects but I can tell you this, cutie, I've been grilled more times than American cheese, and if you ever even *whisper* that I mentioned that film—"

"I won't. And besides, that isn't how I got it."

"Thank God."

"Oh, wow, Donna." Meg shook her head. "Look, I'm really sorry if I got you into trouble. Can I make it up with lunch?"

"Thanks, no. Being seen with you's a hanging offense."

"Oh, boy."

"And you better keep your distance from Keener. I think he's being fingered for this puddle, too."

"Dammit."

"Get away from me, Meg. I'm not kidding."

Meg sighed. From where she was standing at the door, she could see Keener's cubicle. Keener was there, and she watched him as he sat there locking up his desk. He pocketed the key, and then moved toward her.

"Want to talk to you," he said.

"That's news in itself."

"Come on, you." He grabbed her roughly by the arm and yanked her into the hall.

"Police brutality." She looked at him coolly. But then

again, she always looked cool, Keener thought. She was wearing a cool, white Mexican dress and her hair was pulled back from her cool, clean face. Some freckles, like gold dust, powdered her nose.

"Federal brutality," he said. "It's different. We're working under all the damn cutbacks, you know? Our rubber hoses get leaky." He watched her. "Who leaked to you, Meg? And when?"

"You know I can't reveal my—"

"Right." He waved a hand at her. "So how about when? You got any rules about not revealing when?"

"Not that I know of."

"Good."

She was silent.

"All right," he said. "Sunday. When you called me on Sunday—"

"I didn't know Sunday."

"Just fishing?"

"No! I wasn't."

"Uh-huh. So you really did meet him at a party."

"Yes. That's right."

"On Saturday night."

"Yes."

"In Miami."

"Yes."

"Uh-huh. And you thought he was 'nice.' Isn't that what you said?"

"He was."

"He didn't sound too nice in your story."

"Aw, come on, Keener. Are you preaching at me? What the hell's nice got to do with it? A story's a story. I'd write about my own father if—"

"Would you?" He cocked his head at her. "Well, maybe you would. I just wanted to get the chronology straight. On Saturday night he's 'nice' in Miami and on Tuesday he's a 'key suspect,' right? Who told you that, Meg? Your source or your editor?"

She flushed. "It's true."

"Is it?"

"Isn't it?"

"Ah!" He let it sit there, watching as her eyes tried to move from its path. "Which leaves us with Monday.

Somebody fed you something on Monday. Whose little bowl were you eating from, Goldilocks? Rossen's?" Her big blue eyes didn't blink. He nodded, then bluffed. "You were seen in his office on Monday."

She hesitated. "Rossen wasn't there."

"But you were."

She hesitated, "Yes."

"Class dismissed," Keener said.

13.

This time the car on his tail was a Honda. A yellow Honda. It was parked near the house. The tailers were different, younger, but he still couldn't read who they were. Undercover cops, Gallagher reflected, could look about as gamy as the gamiest scuz.

Terry pushed her lips out speculatively. "So what do you think?"

Gallagher shrugged. "They sure look scuzzy."

Turning, she squinted through the window again. "Scuzzy is as scuzzy does. Scuzzy-wuzzy, wuzzy fuzz?"

"Are you stoned?"

"Nope. This is strictly prescription Xanadu. My shrinker keeps sending me on boring little trips. Okay? So I haven't been stoned in a year. Except for the time I was stoned on the streets in a small Italian village for sleeping with a Kraut. Either that was me òr Sophia Loren, I get us mixed up. So anyway, for want of any better kind of trips, I tripped on over here to bake you a cake. Or whatever the condemned man heartily eats—his heart out, I imagine. I imagine if a—"

"Terry!"

"What?"

"Calm down."

"Ha! That's easy for *you* to say. Sorry. I know. I'm blathering. Jesus. If I take enough antidepressants, I blabber till I start depressing everybody else." She looked at him brightly. "I'm fine. How are you?"

"I been better. And you better get away from that window."

Shrugging, she nodded, moving to the couch, and he watched her as she shucked her clogs to the carpet and stretched out her long, sun-coppered legs, staring at the toenails. She'd painted them green. "My rebellion," she said. "Christ. If my father knew my toenails were green, he'd be shipping me directly to the Rest Home. You like that? Rest Home. I think I've got the only family in North America that refers to a rest room as a W.C. and a toilet as a Rest Home." She took a deep breath and looked at him again.

He lit a cigarette. "Hey, look, I don't think you ought to come here for a while. I don't want to worry about both of us, okay? What I mean is, that ain't no pipe dream out there, and if it's Feds you'll get a visit. You don't need that."

She laughed. "It would sure as hell piss my father off, wouldn't it. Jesus. The last time our names were entwined he was practically drummed out of the John Birch Society. He was scared of losing his Blue Cross Membership."

"Terry?"

"What?"

"They might question you anyway."

"Who? The Feds?"

"Yeah."

"So what? Don't worry. I can make remarkably little sense when I try." She grinned, ran her fingers through her long dark hair, and pushed out her lips, wenchy. "Or maybe I'll seduce them. How's that? I mean what's the old proverb? A Fed in the bed is worth two in the bush?"

"Terry?"

"What?"

"Shut up."

"Oh."

"I just want you to protect yourself."

"I'll wear a diaphragm. I've learned, I've learned."

"Now listen, they don't have anything on me. They're fishing, that's all. So if they ask you some questions—"

"What'll they ask me?"

"Do you know Michael Gallagher?"

"Should I tell them I don't?"

"No. Of course not. You tell them you know me. They'll know that you know me or they wouldn't be asking."

"And you call that logic?"

"But they'll ask you, like, 'What is your relationship with him?' "

"Dubious."

"Seriously, Terry."

"Right. We have a seriously dubious relationship. Seriously, Michael. What the hell do I tell them? That you've been my father, my doctor, my banker, my rod and my staff—in fact practically everything on earth but my lover?"

"You tell them we're friends. You don't really see me too often, but we're friends. And if they happen to ask you where I was on the tenth—"

"The tenth?" She paled. "Oh my God. Was that the day—"

"The day Diaz was nabbed."

She was silent for a moment, hunching her shoulders. "What the hell do I tell them?"

"That you don't remember."

She looked up, shaking. "I can't tell the truth, Michael."

"Sure you can. The truth is, you don't remember. You don't remember where *you* were so you don't remember where *I* was. You got it? Repeat it."

"I don't remember."

The following is an edited transcript of a conversation between Agt. R. Keener and Teresa Broadhurst, 6 September. Broadhurst is the daughter of Franklyn Broadhurst (of Broadhurst Steel, and chairman of the Committee for a Better Miami). Teresa is a painter and looks like a model; she's 34, single, and I judge erratic. Interview conducted in Teresa's studio.

KEENER: How long have you known Michael Gallagher?

BROADHURST: How do you even knew that I know him? Were you watching from the Honda?

KEENER: I'm sorry, Miss Broadhurst. I don't understand what you're—

BROADHURST: Maybe you were watching from under the bed. (laughs) Do you ever hide under beds?

KEENER: Not unless the giant Snarks are invading.

BROADHURST: They scare you?

KEENER: Definitely. How long have you known Michael Gallagher?

BROADHURST: Eons. He told me you'd probably know.

KEENER: Would you like to define an eon?

BROADHURST: Since the Stone Age. (laughs) Or the stoned age. (laughs) Something like that.

KEENER: And what's your relationship to Gallagher?

BROADHURST: Friends.

KEENER: Close friends?

BROADHURST: Close.

KEENER: And when was the last time you saw him?

BROADHURST: I don't remember.

KEENER: I see. Do you know his other close friends?

BROADHURST: No. Michael has no other close friends. I'm his closest friend.

KEENER: And his, uh, lover?

BROADHURST: No no no. No.

KEENER: So then if I'd been watching from under the bed . . . ?

BROADHURST: You'd have fallen asleep.

KEENER: Uh-huh. Did you see him on August the 10th?

BROADHURST: I don't remember.

KEENER: You keep an appointment book?

BROADHURST: No. But I keep a disappointment book. It's loaded. You want some tequila or something?

KEENER: No. Thanks. Help yourself if you like.

BROADHURST: (laughs) If I knew how to help myself . . .

KEENER: Yes?

BROADHURST: Ellipsis.

KEENER: Pardon?

BROADHURST: A sentence that ends in three dots. An incomplete sentence that's completely complete. You have a literal mind. I have green toenails. We wouldn't get along.

KEENER: I see.

BROADHURST: And you really showed promise with the Snarks.

KEENER: Yeah. Put me down in your disappointment book. Do you live here?

BROADHURST: No. I live with my parents. In a castle by the sea. I'm often locked in a high tower.

KEENER: Do you live with your parents?

BROADHURST: I just said so, didn't I?

KEENER: Right. Just checking. How close is Gallagher to Santos Malderone?

BROADHURST: How close is Jupiter to Mars?

KEENER: They're not close?

BROADHURST: You win a year's supply of gumshoes. Yes. They're not close. He's close to his other uncle. In Brooklyn. But how close is Brooklyn, you well might ask.

KEENER: What's the other uncle's name?

BROADHURST: I don't remember. In fact, I don't remember anything else.

KEENER: Miss Broadhurst, would you tell me—

BROADHURST: I would if I remembered. But really. I don't remember anything else. So please. if you'll excuse me now, Mister, uh . . .

KEENER: Keener.

BROADHURST: See? I don't even remember your name.

14.

Gallagher opened the door to his office and noted with surprise, after checking it out, that the roof apparently had not fallen in.

Ortega looked at him and said, "Wanna bet?"

Wearily, Gallagher held up a hand. "Don't tell me yet, huh?" He poured himself coffee and took it to his desk.

Ortega was silent, watching, waiting. Ortega had a watching-and-waiting face. He'd been a bantamweight boxer in prison, he'd said, and Gallagher could picture him, edgy and scrappy and dancing in the ring, and then *pow!* When he paced, he punched his own palm.

Gallagher sipped at his coffee, slowly. He lit a cigarette and glanced up at Nicky, who was sitting with the *Chronicle-News* on her lap. He looked back at Ortega.

"Hit me," he said.

"We're hurtin', man. Bad."

"How bad?"

"Minus seven."

Gallagher nodded. "We lost seven accounts."

"Today. And it's only nine-thirty-five. Adding up the week, it's a minus thirteen."

Gallagher sipped at his coffee. "What else. You don't look like you're finished."

"Yeah. We got a case of union trouble."

"Shit."

"You blow away their leader, man, so what you expect?"

"Shit!"

"You got it."

"You think they're gonna wildcat?"

"Wouldn't be surprised. And if they go, the Teamsters go with 'em."

"What the hell. If we got no stock and no customers, who needs the Teamsters?"

Ortega laughed. "Yeah. You got a right-on attitude, amigo. Go with the flow."

"Right down the drain."

Ortega nodded. "There's an old Spanish saying: 'Even stuffed pheasant winds up in the toilet.' "

"Meaning?"

"Life's shit, man. Go with the flow."

McAdam was mad. "I'm waiting," he said. "I'm waiting for your major Gallagher piece and where the hell were you?"

"In court. I thought you'd want the dope case story. Two dozen guys got sentenced to—"

"Fuck 'em. What I want is Gallagher. I had to have Chalmers do a fill piece this morning. Are you on it or not?"

"I'm on it," Meg said.

"I want it for Sunday. Three thousand words."

"Fine. And while I'm up I'll write *War and Peace.*"

"I'll settle for war. So make it a thousand."

"Good," Meg nodded. "Which leaves me only nine hundred ninety-two to go. I mean, so far I've spoken to four friends of Gallagher's and each of them handed me two words apiece. And I'll give you a hint, they were not 'no comment.' "

"Try Gallagher."

"He thinks I've already tried him. And convicted him. Remember?"

"Try him again."

Meg grabbed a copy of the morning's edition and carefully looked over Chalmers copy. The headline was a cutesy: LIKE FATHER LIKE SON? with a picture of each, but the article itself was devoted to "Tommy: His Flashy Career in Florida Crime." The parallels to Michael included the fact that

On Tuesday, Mr. Gallagher stormed through the newsroom of the *Chronicle-News,* angrily demanding to face his accuser, but when asked if he could prove the accusations were false, he merely exploded with evasive invective. "I don't have to prove an (expletive deleted) thing!"

said Mr. Gallagher, echoing exactly the words
of his father, who, when indicted in 1970 for
conspiracy and fraud involving IDU funds,
told . . .

Well . . . he'd said that, she had to admit. He'd even,
in fact, "exploded" with it. Still, the tone of what had
happened was wrong.

Lighting a cigarette, she thought about that. What
Chalmers had written was not really just.

And it was just what she needed.

Gallagher's secretary answered the phone in a voice
that could have frozen a hot potato, which was clearly
what she thought a call from Meg Carter was.

Meg was left to cool in the limbo of Hold. She doodled
in her notebook and tried to remember exactly what she'd
read about Nicole Peralta. Keener had called her "attractive, divorced." Gallagher's neighbor had called her a redhead, among other things, and had also implied she had
"ten-gallon jugs," and added, "she stays with Gallagher a
lot." Meg began to wonder what the woman was like. Or
what Gallagher's taste in women was like.

His voice made her jump—a sudden, brisk, "So what
do you want?"

"To apologize," she said quickly.

He was silent.

"I thought the article this morning was, well . . . un-
fair."

"Oh you did." He laughed, and repeated it to someone.
To Nicole?

"So I wanted—I mean, I wondered—I mean, I thought
it would only be fair to—well . . . you know—to be fair."

He was silent.

"What I mean is, I think it would be fair if we heard
your side of it."

He was silent. She could hear him light a cigarette.
"You want to listen to me, huh?"

"Exactly. Yes. I'll record it so—"

"Oh, no! I won't talk to any goddam machines. If I
want to sit around and talk to a machine, I'll talk to the
goddam washing machine. Are you a machine?"

"I don't think so."

"Feel up your back. Is there a key?"

She laughed.

"Another test is, you ever eat lunch?"

"Daily."

"Good. Then I'll pick you up at noon. It's a red T-bird. The one with Diaz's blood on the hood."

"Quick," Meg said. "Where's the pin-recorder, Mac?"

"What do you want with—"

"I'm having lunch with Gallagher."

"Yeah? No kidding. How'd you do that?"

"I called and he asked me."

"Hey. Hot damn," McAdam said, grinning. "Now look, don't worry, you can handle it, kid. You'll play him like a harp and he'll think you're an angel. Wait a second. Why are you—"

"Give me your penknife."

"Jesus. You think you need a weapon?"

"Of course not, Mac. What could happen at a lunch?"

"I don't know. It depends where you happen to lunch. For instance, a picnic on the edge of a cliff—"

"The knife," she said flatly, and used it to punch a really heartrending hole in the tailored lapel of her blue linen blazer.

McAdam fumbled in the drawer of his desk and produced a recorder, buried in a fake Marlboro pack, and attached by a wire to a stickpin mike. "So what's with the Mata Hari routine? Doesn't he know you're gonna write about him?"

"Nope. I mean, he didn't ask." She threaded the mike through the hole in her lapel and buried the receiver in an inside pocket. "And since he didn't ask me, I didn't have to lie. The only thing he asked me was not to record him. And I didn't really answer."

McAdam shook his head. "I don't like it. I don't like it. Listen, when I first got into this business, a wise old fella named Hammy Roginsky taught me the three basic rules of survival: never make fun of a seven-foot man, never make love to a sore that won't heal, and never make a promise to a guy in the mob if you don't intend to keep it."

"Mac, I repeat. What could happen at a lunch? Worse

comes to worst, he could toss a bowl of spinach salad at my head."

"I don't like it. I'm sending Casey to cover you."

"That'll be subtle. Mr. Gallagher, I'd like you to meet my father. Ignore those cameras slung around his neck, he's a tourist."

"I'll see he stays twenty feet behind you. If he catches any long-lens stuff, that's a plus. I don't care about the pictures, I want to have someone who'll know where you are. This is no kidding, Megan. Don't play around. This guy could be a killer."

Meg cocked her head. "Do you really think so?"

"Christ," McAdam frowned. "If *not*, what the hell have we been writing about?" He turned. "Hey, Casey!" he bellowed. "C'mere!"

15.

Outside, once again, the heat was amazing. Coming from the winter of the air-conditioned room, she could feel it knock her backwards like an actual blow. She retreated to the lobby and waited, watching through the big glass doors for the Thunderbird "with Diaz's blood on the hood."

Terrific.

McAdam had really got her scared, and nasty little images fluttered in her head. According to the catalog of popular wisdom, the Mafia never wreaked vengeance on the press, but the footnotes were loaded with exceptions to the rule.

A vicious explosion stopped traffic today as intrepid Meg Carter of the *Chronicle-News* turned the ignition of her blue-and-white Vega and exploded into fragments at the curb in front of Saks. Miss Carter will remain on display throughout the week on the window with the camisole by Yves Saint-Laurent (sizes 4–14, $300).

A horn honked loudly. She roused herself and looked through the window at the street; at the bright red Thunderbird waiting at the curb; at Casey's Volkswagon waiting at the corner.

"Sorry. The traffic was murder," he said. He held the door open from inside the car and slid back over to the driver's seat. Music was playing on a tape deck: "Luck Be A Lady," and she wondered if his playing *Guys and Dolls* was a joke. His expression offered no indication of humor. His eyes weren't icy, they were simply disinterested; he kept them on the road. His face was impassive, a poker player's face. He was dressed in a T-shirt and

weathered-looking jeans, but alligator sandals. The
Touch, she decided, of self-conscious Class.

It was cool in the car. She turned around quickly and
glanced through the window. Casey was there, tailgating.
Dumb. She looked up at Gallagher, who hadn't seemed to
notice, and noticed the clean hard lines of his face, the
scar (very small) on the edge of his temple, the slant of
his eyebrows, the cleft in his chin, the hang-tough cigarette stuck in his mouth—the profile, she thought, of a
suspected killer.

"How long you get for lunch?" he said.

"Long as I want."

He shrugged. "Good job."

She nodded. "I guess."

He turned onto Biscayne Boulevard from Flagler, and
headed down the coast.

She said, "Where are we going?"

He looked at her. "To lunch."

She nodded. "Oh. Where?" she said.

"Boat club."

"Oh," she said.

His eyes flicked up to the rear-view mirror. "Either
I've got a new friend or you've got an old one."

"What?"

"The old guy in the gray VW. He's tailing us. Friend
of yours?"

She felt herself flush. "Who would be tailing me?"

He nodded, "Right," and stepped on the pedal. She
thought she saw the flicker of a smile on his lips.

He parked in the lot of the Shoreham Marina in front
of the boat club. He didn't try to open the door for her
this time, but walked around quickly to the back of the
car and extracted a big brown bag from the trunk.

Standing in the sun again, Meg felt the heat and the
reassuring presence of shoot-'em-up Casey, who looked,
in his loud plaid polyester suit, about as inconspicuous as
bats in the ointment.

Gallagher seemed to check quickly through the lot,
more or less squinting at a pale yellow Honda. "You
coming?" he said.

"Isn't the restaurant there?" She pointed.

"And there." He pointed at the brown paper bag. "Picnic," he said.

She nodded. "Oh." *For instance, a picnic on the edge of a cliff,* McAdam had said. "Where?"

"You don't like surprises much, do you?" He started to lead her on the path toward the pier.

"Mostly," she said, "the surprises I get run along the lines of finding spiders in my shoe."

He pointed at the bag again. "Curds and whey."

"What?"

"Miss Muffet."

"Oh." She felt stupid.

"And what the hell's a tuffet?"

"I don't know," she said.

"I thought you knew everything."

"No," she said, "you didn't."

They were walking very quickly down a very long pier, and she was suddenly conscious of the tingle of her nerves. Or the tingle of something. She glanced at the bay. The yachts, slick and curried and rocking in their slips, looked arrogant as thoroughbreds champing in their stalls.

She was perishing of heat. The bugged linen blazer was sticking to her back. And so was Casey. If he got any closer he'd be tripping on her heels, but Gallagher seemed to be oblivious again.

A rather grimy old man who looked like he hired out to swab people's decks waved cheerfully at Gallagher. " 'Lo there," he said.

"How'd the fishin go, Charlie?"

"Hell, ya don't need another fish story, do ya?"

Gallagher laughed. "Not this week, I don't." He turned to her, stopping, and extended his arm. It pointed at the prow of an old wooden speedboat. A good-looking old— maybe antique—with its mahogany hull and its shiny brass rail. "Figured we'd picnic on the water," he said, and she watched as he jumped and landed on the cockpit. He dumped the groceries and turned to her. "I think you'd better toss me your shoes."

She stared at him.

"I'll give you some cement ones instead."

She stared at him. His eyes were a deep sea blue and she wondered if he'd drown her, one way or the other.

He shook his head at her slowly. "Lady, you want to make a jump in those spikes . . ."

"Oh," she said, nodding rather dumbly at her shoes, and then looked back at Casey, who'd stopped in his tracks. She turned back to Gallagher.

"You scared?" he said.

"No! Of what?"

He held his hands out and grabbed her by the waist and lifted her, shoes and all, to the deck. He put her down quickly. "For a second there I thought you might be scared about sharks. Sit." He pointed at a bolted-down chair, and before she had a chance to think of anything to say, he'd started a motor that was catching with a roar, and then a second motor started, till it sounded like a 747 taking off, and then suddenly they seemed to be flying on the water, the boat planing high about the glittering surface and throwing up a silver-white plumage in its wake. The speed was thrilling; the wind whipped her hair, and she found herself grinning and clutching at the bottom of her white cotton skirt, which the wind kept lifting like a flag of surrender. He was standing at the wheel, though he could have been sitting, and she caught herself staring at his firm brown arms, unmoving, though the wheel was almost fighting with his hands, and they had to be powerful to hold it so steady, and she found herself wondering what it would be like to be held by those arms. She looked away quickly. It was frightening to feel such attraction to the man.

The motors roared on; she started to wonder where the hell he was taking her.

"How far out are we?" she yelled.

"Not far."

"How fast are we going?" she tried.

"Figure only . . ." But she seemed to lose the tail of the sentence to the wind.

The boat kept moving at a speed she couldn't figure.

"How old is this thing?"

"Me? Forty-seven."

"No! The boat!"

"Oh! Same thing. Built in 'thirty-four."

"Pretty fast engines!"

He laughed against the wind, threw his head back and laughed, and for a moment he almost seemed to glitter like the water. Then suddenly she felt the boat slowing; it stopped. He turned and looked at her. The silence was stunning. She sat there holding it, afraid to break it, as though it were some kind of precious piece of glass that could never be mended. They were all alone in a big blue world.

"God, it's quiet," she finally said.

He nodded. "Yeah."

"How far out are we?"

"Five, six miles."

"Oh."

"No sharks."

She flushed.

"And the engines are new."

"Oh."

"Take your jacket off. Relax. I'll get lunch."

He picked up the bag and disappeared down the hatch.

There wasn't much breeze, and she was roasting again. She fumbled in her handbag and found a few hairpins; twisting her hair into a messy little topknot, she pinned it into place.

"Hey, do you need any help there?" she hollered.

"Nope." He appeared with a bottle and some glasses. She looked at the bottle. "That's lunch?"

"That's right. Hell, I figured if I got you really soused you'd confess you killed Diaz. No, it's not lunch. Lunch is still below. I got two hands, lady." He was pouring the wine.

"Meg."

"Lady Meg." He handed her a glass.

It was wonderfully icy cold in her hand. She sipped it. "Hey, this is terrific," she said.

"Clos Blanc de Vougeot."

"Is that good?"

He squinted at her. "What do you mean, 'is that good?' You're drinking it. Is it?"

She nodded.

"Well, it oughtta be. Three hundred sixty-seven smackers a case. Wholesale."

"Really?"

"Two bucks a bottle. What is it with you? You either like it or you don't. You need a label to tell you if you like it, you're in trouble."

She flushed. "I know exactly what *I* like," she said. "I just wanted to know what *you* like. I mean, I figured you're an expert. Aren't you?"

He grinned at her and lifted his glass. "Smooth sailing," he said, and she couldn't tell if that had been a label or a toast.

"Was this your father's boat?"

"Yeah."

"The one he took to Cuba?"

"You been doin your homework. No, the one he took to Cuba was a yacht. He lost it in a poker game to Bugsy Siegel. This is the one he ran whiskey in, though."

"Wait. I thought you said it was built in thirty-four."

"So?"

"Prohibition was gone in thirty-three."

"Legally it was. But Tommy never paid much attention to the law."

She laughed.

"Hell, he figured if he liked doin something, he should do it. So he kept on doin it. Rode out at midnight and back before dawn with a hold full of whisky. No tax stamps. It used to work out pretty good."

She remembered the story now and added, "Till he went to jail for it."

"Hell. That didn't stop him. It just made him smarter."

"How about you?"

"What about me?"

"Are you smart about it?"

"Yeah. I was smart enough to not ever try it."

She looked at him doubtfully. "Why not? It sounds like you could make a lot of money."

"Yeah. You could also lose a lot of time. Aren't you hot in that jacket?"

"Oh no," she said. "No. I'm fine. Are you saying you were never in the business?"

"That's right." He grinned again. "Sorry," he said.

"Are you?"

He looked up quickly. "Sometimes. Yeah. When business is bad. And when I'm out here sometimes, and I wonder what it might've been like on the run . . . and livin high."

"So you have felt tempted."

"Hey, you ever been tempted to shoplift? I bet you haven't done it, but I bet you been tempted. Tempted doesn't count. Besides, I never really had any kind of choice. Tommy said no. And when Tommy said no, he meant no." He lit a cigarette. "Sure you're not hot?"

"I'm fine." She'd been pressing the wine glass to her face. "People say—"

"You're kinda sweatin in the Blanc de Vougeot."

"No, really. I'm fine."

"Nice pin. Is it good?"

"What?"

"Is it good jewelry."

"Oh."

"I don't know about jewelry."

"Oh. Well, it's just kind of . . . junky."

"Yeah. Go on. People say what?"

"That your father ran Miami."

"Hell, no. He just had a lot of friends and relations."

"Do you?"

He tipped his chair back. "Not the kind you mean."

"A wife?"

"Once. Good-lookin', but no friend a' mine. You gettin hungry? I am." He stood abruptly, and went down below.

She heard him making plate-banging noises in the galley, and suddenly remembered that she hadn't turned the goddam tape recorder on. She moaned out loud and reached into the inside pocket for the switch. Her blouse was soaked, and she wondered if she'd maybe electrocute herself when she turned the thing on.

He'd changed to a bathing suit. He stood in front of her with two white plates and the grocery bag, and his body. She watched his body while he moved. It was a body, all right.

"Chicken?"

She looked at him. "What?"

"I got a chicken sandwich and a burger. I figured you were probably the chicken-sandwich type."

"Fine," she said. He handed her the sandwich on a plate, but still wrapped in its foil. The pickle had been leaking on the soggy white bread. "I think we were discussing your wife," she said.

"No. We finished with her. How about you. How come you're not married?"

"Maybe I am."

"You don't wear a ring."

"Ever heard of Liberation?"

He poured himself some wine. "Most of them are ugly."

"Thanks. I think." She bit into her sandwich. Chicken slid out and landed on her skirt. She sighed and put it back on the plate. "I'm divorced," she said quickly.

"What happened? He hate sloppy eaters?"

She laughed. "Who says it was him did the leaving?"

He nodded. "How long you been divorced?"

"Mmm. Seven years."

"Seven . . . *years?* How old are you?"

"Well . . . I don't think I'll tell you."

"Bullshit."

"I'm twenty-seven."

He squinted. "Hold it. You mean you're divorced at *twenty?* How the hell could you be divorced at twenty?"

"Easy. You marry bad at nineteen."

"And then what?"

"You get divorced at twenty."

He put down his burger. "I mean after the divorce. Then what did you do?"

"I finished college."

"And then what?"

She shrugged. "I looked for a job. I always had this thing about doing the news."

"You mean write it."

"No. I mean do it. You know, do it."

"No. I don't know."

"I mean, 'This is Meg Carter at Rockefeller Center and, as you can see, the—' "

"Oh. Do it. You mean they don't write it? On television? They just . . . *do* it?"

"Well, it depends."

"Uh-huh. So what happened?"

"I did it. Got a job on a six o'clock news."

"Like that?" He snapped his fingers.

"Like that."

"Comes easy, huh?"

She shrugged, took another sip of her wine. "It was awful," she said. "The anchorman—Chuck?—was this total meatball. He called me Meg-Meg. Jesus. You believe that? On the air! Meg-Meg. And sometimes Nut-Meg. And then there were times it was Daisy Meg. Like some farty little pun about Daisy Mae."

He lit a cigarette. "Farty. That's nice. You like talkin like that?"

"What's the matter with it?"

"Well, it's inapt, for one thing. Christ. How the hell could a pun be farty?"

She shrugged. "I don't know. If it ate a lot of beans?"

He laughed. "Tough-guy."

"Yeah. That's me. Let's talk about you."

He nodded. "All right. I got nothin to hide. What do you want to know?"

"To start with, the obvious. What did it feel like, I mean as a kid, to be the son of a—" She stopped.

"Of a what?"

"Of a reputed figure in organized crime."

"You mean of a hood? It was embarrassing sometimes." He shrugged. "I don't know. There were kids who couldn't play with me. Their mommies wouldn't let them."

"Oh."

"Aside from that, it wasn't too bad. What else?"

She thought. "How'd you feel about your father?"

"Hell, I don't know. He was, uh, my father. He was away a lot."

"On business?"

He laughed. "I mean Away. In jail."

"Oh. Was that hard on your mother?"

"Nope. She was dead. She died when I was three. When Tommy went to jail, I went to live with his sister. In Brooklyn. Her and her husband took me in. I was fifteen, I guess. Charlie ran a laundry. An Irish laundry. Christ, you want to talk about growing up clean. After

school I used to work at these giant vats. Boiling soap.
Jesus." He laughed. "And when Tommy got out, I was
over in Seoul."

"In soul?"

"South Korea. Before your time."

"Oh."

"Literally. No. You were one."

"And then what? After the army?"

"School. On the G.I. Bill. For, uh—hell, I guess I
lasted four or five months. I thought it was bullshit. Then
I tried to be an actor."

"Were you good?"

"I don't know. I was too broke to notice. After that,
I ran a bar for a while. I *was* good at that. And then I
got married and worked for her father."

"How long were you married?"

"Longer than you."

"Who wasn't? How long?"

"Twelve years. I got a daughter. Sixteen."

"Where is she?"

"At a boarding school. In France. Her mother has pre-
tensions."

"And what kind of business—"

"Boats. I sold boats. If that was the question. Mari-
anne's father had a boat-selling business." He suddenly
grinned. "Jesus. I really am duller than shit, aren't I."

"No. I just wondered . . ."

"What?"

"Well, you are kind of *straight*. How'd you get so
straight?"

He reached for the bottle. "Give me your glass and
I'll give you a story." She held out her glass. "When I was
fourteen"—he poured some more wine—"me and these
two other guys swiped a car. Not for keeps, just for fun.
Joyriding, right? So anyway, Tommy finds out that we did
it. So he takes me to this Godforsaken strip of the beach.
To this shack. Dirt basement. Locked me in and left.
Three days."

She frowned at him. "And who was he to preach?"

"Hey, he wasn't preaching. He just said, Look, kid,
you want to be a thief, you better know what it's like."

She studied him. "You're something, Gallagher. You know? So you learned your lesson."

He nodded. "Learned a lot of good lessons from Tommy. What else you want to know?"

"As much as you'll tell me. I really meant it. I want to be fair."

He nodded again. "One of those real up-front ladies." Something in his voice made her wary.

"I try to be."

"Then who's the old guy in the gray VW." He leaned forward suddenly and yanked her lapel. *"And who the hell am I talkin to there?"*

For a second they were frozen, both of them, his hand still clutching her jacket. And she wondered what he'd do. He could as easily slug her as throw her to the sea.

What he did was release her and then start to laugh. "Sharpie," he said. "Jesus." He shrugged. "And most of what you've got there's a whole lot of sweat and your own life story."

She started to giggle, and then couldn't stop.

He was shaking his head at her.

"Well . . ." she said. "What would you suggest we do now?"

"There's some bathing suits below. In the locker."

She hesitated, almost said no, and then nodded instead and wondered, on the way to the cabin below, if the suits would be Nicky's and whether they'd fit. Not if Nicky had "ten-gallon jugs."

The cabin was bigger than she'd thought it would be, with shined brass lanterns and mahogany walls. There was a bed, which she noticed was the first thing she noticed, and a couple of facing leather banquettes with a table that would drop into place between them. There were built-in mahogany bookshelves on the wall, with an antique captain's desk fitted beneath; she looked at the book titles. Books on the sea: Melville, Heyerdahl, Conrad, Cousteau, and a paperback collection of Travis McGees that seemed to form a bridge between the deeper, more exotic puzzles of the sea and the mysteries of Hammett, Chandler, and Cain. A hardcover copy of *The Godfather*, stuck at an angle on the shelf, amused her, and something made her open it. The inside cover was inscribed in a bold, backhand writing in purplish ink:

From the Palm Beach Heiress with
lurid love—

Always,
T.

She put it back quickly, not liking the tickle of the feeling it gave her. She did not like to think that in less than an hour she could feel . . . anything, and certainly not for a man who half-scared her. Chemistry. A subject that belonged on the shelf with the other mysteries.

"You lost or just snooping?" His voice drifted down.

"If those are the only choices, I'm lost."

She heard him laughing.

"The guns are in the closet. The Tommy guns, I mean. The Mike gun's in the desk."

"Funny," she said. "And where are the bathing suits?"

"Keep snooping," he yelled. "You'll find them."

16.

All in all, he figured, it was going just fine. He'd painted himself as an open, agreeable, but not stupid fellow, and meanwhile he'd painted her into a corner. He poured some more wine, killing the bottle. What he hadn't counted on was finding her even remotely attractive, but that's what he found her: remotely attractive. Attractive, but remote. Emotional virgin. One of those snappy little tease-toy ladies. A barbed Barbie Doll. Well, what the hell.

She appeared wearing Terry's little blue and white suit. She wore it very well. She'd braided her hair and she stood in a yellow dazzle of sun and looked at him uncertainly, shrugging.

"Lovely," he said, and watched as she smiled. He went into the cockpit and brought out some lotion. He tossed it to her. "White-meat turkey," he said, and sprawled on the terry cloth mat on the deck.

"How's the water?" she said.

"Shark infested."

"Really?"

"I don't know. But it's cold."

"I don't know if I care." She dived into the water. Gutsy, anyway. She came up spluttering and goose-pimpled. "Forget it. I care. Christ." She shivered and stretched on the other sun-mat beside him and studied him. He glanced at her and then closed his eyes. They were silent for a moment. For a moment, he thought it was still going fine. Then she said abruptly, "If you knew I was bugging you, I guess you were lying."

He opened his eyes again.

"I mean, all the stuff about being so clean."

He laughed, harshly. "Christ. You got a nasty mind, you know that? It's the Shaunessey Laundry on DeKalb Street. Try it. I mean, shit, send your mind there and get it cleaned up."

She flushed again.

"You really think I did Diaz?"

"It's a hot possibility."

"Hey, you don't *know* the kind of guy that did Diaz. Go get on a boat with *those* guys, Sharpie."

"Then why is the Strike Force after you?"

"Exactly," he said. "They got nothin. They want somethin, but they got nothin. And the thing is, I need to know who wants what. And to know that, I gotta know who was your source."

"I can't tell you that."

"Right. You want to know why I talked to you, lady? I wanted you to get my obituary straight."

She looked startled for a moment, then shrugged. "You're just trying to scare me."

He laughed. "Nothin scares you, right?" He rolled over on his stomach. "Someone wants to get me, you understand that? I don't know. So maybe they do think I did it. My old man was thick with McKee and Cavaletti. And Santos isn't known as The Eel for nothin. He's slippery. I don't know. So maybe they're just leaning on me. Or maybe the guys who did Diaz are setting me up. Or maybe it's just an old enemy of Tommy's being cute for the sheer fucking hell of it. I don't know. But you do. 'Knowledgeable sources.' Who the hell's that?"

She said nothing.

"Let's get it straight, okay? I'm being blackmailed by a guy who can hide behind Amendments. And you're the one that's writing up the blackmail notes. Don't you see it?"

She said nothing.

"You don't see it," he said. "All you can see is your name on the byline. Hot-shot reporter. You're a *stooge*, dummy. They're using you, too."

She said nothing.

He turned away, grunting disgust.

They were both silent.

Finally she said, "Look, if they clear you, I'll write that too."

"Yeah. Terrific. Let me tell you something, lady. I knew a guy in Brooklyn got indicted for murder. And ten years later he's still gettin looked at from corners of the eyes.

See, people just remember he's connected with a murder.
They forget he was innocent. Even though the paper
printed it—lovely—on page ninety-three."

She looked away from him.

He whistled under his breath. A chopper was buzzing
around in the air. He stood, abruptly. "We better get
goin. No use messin up the whole afternoon."

She cocked her head at him. "Why did you do this?
The boat, the picnic . . ."

"Yeah. It was a setup. I didn't want to let you walk
away from some diner before I got my answers." He shook
his head wryly. "Good strategy, huh?" He headed for the
cockpit. "You better get dressed." He looked at her,
frowned, and looked up at the sky. It was a cop chopper,
practically buzzing the deck.

A P.A. voice hollered down, "Meg Carter?" and Gallagher watched as she hollered back. "Yes!"

"You all right?" the cop bellowed.

She nodded. "I'm fine!"

"Okay!" and the chopper pulled up and away.

"I'm sorry," she said, but he was starting the motor.

"Can't hear you."

"The photographer must have got worried."

He started the second motor.

She stood there. "I'm really sorry," she said.

He gave it full throttle, and the boat thundered off.

She peeled the suit off and hung it up to dry on the
faucet of the shower.

She wasn't in a hurry to get back to the deck, and she
wasn't really sure what she thought of him anyway. The
thing was, she'd really believed him for a while. She'd
believed he was clean. From the laundry on DeKalb
Street right up to now. But then he'd admitted that the
day was a setup. So maybe he'd been lying. Even though
he'd told her hotly that he hadn't.

The old riddle: The Blackfoot Indian and the Whitefoot Indian. The Blackfoot Indians never tell the truth
and the Whitefoot Indians never tell a lie. So you ask
an Indian, "Which one are you, a Truthful Whitefoot or
a Lying Blackfoot?" and the Indian tells you, "I'm a
Truthful Whitefoot."

So which one is he?

She reached for her dress and, zipping it, wandered back into the cabin.

Who are you, Michael Gallagher?

She looked at his books, at the way he'd folded his clothes on the chair, and she thought about the way he looked and moved and sounded, and the way he laughed when he laughed, and she wanted to believe he'd been telling the truth.

She'd left her handbag on the top of the desk—a pretty little desk, with wine-colored leather on the lift-up top. She hesitated, staring at the desk for a moment and tracing a finger on the edge of her lip.

All's fair in love in war.

I'll settle for war, McAdam had said.

She opened the desk.

Inside was a jumble of letters and bills. A locked metal box. A note—in the same backhand writing and purple ink that she'd seen in the book:

Michael—

Missed you. The Feds came to see me. I think I goofed about a couple of things, but I remembered not to remember the 10th. Okay?

(I remembered the Alamo.)

T.

17.

"I got a couple of things here," Hamilton said. He was holding an envelope.

"Are they smaller than an envelope?" Keener drank some coffee from a styrofoam cup, then hurtled the cup, still full, at a metal basket on the floor. "Dunk shot," he said. "Go on." He fumbled for a match on the desk.

"Our friend's been having an interesting day."

"Make me jealous," Keener said.

Hamilton shrugged. "I guess that comes second. First, he's got Malderone's goons on his tail."

"Still." Keener nodded. "They lose another Buick?"

"Not that I know of. I figure those soldiers must've lost a few stripes. Or got a few brains. Today they had a three-car changeable tail."

"They've been watching the cop shows."

"Yeah. The old ones," Hamilton said. "When the cops had the money for a three-car tail."

"You're right. That went out with 'Naked City.' "

"And speaking of naked city—" Hamilton tossed the envelope at Keener, a manilla envelope, five by seven.

Keener opened it. He hadn't found a match and the unlit cigarette was stuck in his mouth; he let it fall out. "Well, well." In glossy, clear, black-and-white blowups, Michael Gallagher and Megan Carter lay side by side on the deck of a boat. Keener looked up. "It's a copter shot."

"Yeah. A guy named Casey called the Coast Guard, yet. He thought she'd been kidnapped."

"Who took the picture?"

"Cops. They heard 'Gallagher' and 'kidnap' and they flew to the rescue with gun and camera. She said she was fine."

Keener looked up again. "As any fool can see. What was going on?"

Hamilton shrugged. "I don't know, but this Casey guy tailed her from the office. So it must've been business."

"Saigon Sue Striking Again."

"I figure."

"Then we'll read it in the paper tomorrow. What else've you got?"

"Teresa Broadhurst."

"How about a light?"

"You lose another lighter?"

"Another sixty-nine cents down the drain." Keener caught the matchbook and used it. "Go on."

"She went to Gallagher's boat. She got there maybe half an hour before he did and left before he came."

"Who was on stakeout?"

"Cole. He said she just went into the cabin and came back out again five minutes later. Doesn't sound important, but I thought you'd want to know."

"So she has her own key."

"Oh. I guess."

Keener blew a smoke ring and watched it. "I think I'm gonna check the lady out."

"For what?"

"For the hell of it. I don't know for what. Hunch. I got a hunch she knows more than she's saying. Or less." Keener shrugged. "She's a gooney bird, that one. How're you coming with the news of the fire?"

"Gallagher was out of town when it happened. Got back the next morning."

"Where was he?"

"On a weekend with Nicky Peralta. They were visiting her brother in Jacksonville. And by the way, that's where she was on the tenth."

"You talk to her?"

"No. To her mother. I'm still typing the report."

"Let me see it."

McAdam tossed the picture on her desk. "Have fun?" he said dryly.

She looked at it and flushed. "Where did you—"

"I bought it from a mercenary cop. So I hope you got a mighty good story."

"I don't get it," she said. "Why did you—"

"Why? Because if I didn't buy it, the *Times-Gazette* would. Or one of those supermarket toilet papers. Headline: 'Reporter Lies Down on the Job.' "

"Oh."

He shook his head at her. "Just tell me this isn't what it looks like."

"What does it look like?"

"Reporter Lies Down on the Job."

"It isn't what it looks like."

"Prove it. What's the story?"

She thought it over carefully. "Well . . . I'm not really sure what I think. I'm kind of—"

"Hey! Did I ask you what you think? I just asked you for a story. Two thousand words."

"A thousand, you said."

He picked up the picture. "That was seven hundred bucks ago. Look, you were out there for three solid hours. If you weren't playing kissy-face, he must've said something. I want it. Or I want my money back."

"You're kidding!"

"I don't know. Wanna try me?"

"Mac?"

He turned.

"I need an extension. I need some more time to really check out the facts. I can't do it all between tonight and tomorrow."

He looked at her appraisingly. "How long'll it take?"

"As long as it takes."

"That isn't any answer."

"It's the only one I've got."

"Tuesday," he said. "That'll give you three days."

"It won't be enough."

"Bullshit!" he said. "God made the goddam universe in six. I think you can make a damn deadline in three!"

McAdam walked off.

"Library."

"Jimmy? Meg Carter here."

"And what can I do for you, Meg o' my heart?"

"Well, it's a toughy, but I figured you could help. I need to find a file."

"Well, that isn't tough. What file do you need?"

"I don't know."

"You don't know?"

"That's what's tough. It's a Palm Beach heiress whose name begins with *T*. Her first name."

"Oh." He made a few denture-clicking sounds with his tongue, thinking. "Is there anything else you know about her?"

"I'm not even sure she's a Palm Beach heiress. It might've been a joke."

"I see. Can you give me a clue about her age?"

Meg thought it over. "She's old enough to know about lurid love."

"These days, I guess that means she's over six. Is there any special subject she's connected to maybe? Charity? Art?"

"Gallagher?"

"Oh. Well, there's nothing in the Gallagher file, and it's all cross-referenced, so that doesn't help. On the other hand, we only file our own clippings. So if something was written up in some other paper . . ." He sighed. "I'll look around and see what I can find."

"You're a love."

"Ah yes." He laughed in her ear. "I know it and you know it, but would you please tell it to Suzanne Somers?"

Gallagher moaned and punched at the button that killed the alarm. He couldn't think of any particular reason for opening his eyes, so he left them as they were, put a pillow on his head, and said, "Wake me when it's over."

Nobody answered.

He opened his eyes and found Nicky was gone, or at least not there. He listened, heard her moving around in the kitchen, humming, and even caught the sudden aroma of bacon.

The idea that she was out there fixing him bacon propelled him from the bedroom to as far as the hall, where the morning's paper was lying on the floor. Even from the distance, he could see the headline (REAGAN WON'T VETO) and he didn't miss the humor in the feeling of relief that Reagan had replaced him as The Story of the Day. On the other hand, he didn't want to look any further. Carter would have written up yesterday's lunch, and they hadn't exactly parted as pals.

In the kitchen, Nicky looked up from the stove. She was already dressed in a pink cotton dress and pink leather sandals with towering heels, and she'd carefully plaited her auburn hair into one single braid that dangled to her waist. He noticed the wall phone had been left off the hook.

"What's with the phone?"

"Good morning," she said.

He nodded. "Good morning, you look beautiful, I love you for fixing my breakfast, and what's with the phone?"

"Eat. Have some coffee."

"I haven't brushed my teeth."

"The coffee won't care." She handed him a coffee cup and filled it.

"Sit down."

"The bacon'll burn."

"Sit down, Pancho." He pointed. "The phone."

"Obscene callers?"

"For me or for you?"

"Mine I get at home." She was turning the bacon.

"What did who say?"

"You don't want to hear this."

"I know I don't."

"First fill your stomach. I got biscuits in the—"

"Nicky?"

She shrugged. "A man said to tell you to go back where you came from. To Italy."

"To Italy?" Gallagher laughed.

"It gets funnier. Another man called and he told me to tell you to check your garage. So I checked your garage. There's a very dead pigeon hanging from the door."

"Aw, Jesus."

"And then on my way to the house, your wonderful neighbor told me to go back to Mexico, so I told him I come from Cuba, so he told me to go back to San Juan." She was putting the bacon on a napkin to drain. "I've been trying to decide if that's funny or not. But I'll give you the *good* news."

"There's good news?"

"Yeah. No news. You're not in the paper today."

*   *   *

Keener checked the Saturday *Chronicle-News,* found nothing on Gallagher, and wondered what it meant. Maybe they were saving him, like roast turkey, for a Sunday feast.

At noon, after dropping off his shirts at the laundry, he headed down south on the Dixie Highway for the palmy little campus of Miami U.

The library there was cool, half-empty, and, unlike the libraries run by the city, allowed you to smoke.

He picked a table at the back of the room, lit a cigarette, and started to check through the last dozen volumes of the *Annual Index of the Chronicle-News.* There were two items on Teresa Broadhurst. The first one was current (May 17, 26:2) and the second was old: 1970 (Nov. 22, 31:2): HEIRESS IN CRASH.

The *Times-Gazette* had a listing for the crash, but no other mention of Teresa Broadhurst.

Keener stubbed his cigarette and browsed through the shelves. Library work, being slow and unthrilling, was hardly ever mentioned in the shoot-'em-up thrillers, but actual agents found it useful and discreet, a way to learn the obvious without leaving tracks.

While he waited for his order to arrive at the call-desk, he checked a few volumes of *Who's Who In Finance* and *Who Was Who,* and learned Franklyn Broadhurst was a fifth generation son of a bitch. He'd been married to the now-dead Mary Lou Potter, had a son named Walker who'd been killed in the Tet offensive, and a daughter, Teresa. His politics apparently were far to the right, a genetic proclivity undoubtedly inherited from Hamilton Broadhurst, original founder of Broadhurst Steel, who'd frittered his octogenarian years sending money to Franco and otherwise to squadrons of Pinkerton goons for the purpose of busting up the Steelworkers' union.

A girl with a pony tail and very bad acne delivered the paper and the boxes of film. "I just maybe thought you forgot them," she said.

Keener thanked her and she smiled, and then blushed and retreated, colliding with the corner of a chair.

Keener felt touched. Courage, he reflected, was a relative thing. There ought to be Bronze Stars awarded for valor to fat girls with acne who could get themselves to walk across library floors in the face of the devastating guns of indifference.

He threaded the microfilm into the reader and cranked it till he got to November 22, page 31:

HEIRESS IN CRASH

And she sure as hell was.

What she'd crashed was a half-million dollar Piaggio —a twin-engined, customized, Italian-made plane.

> The 23-year-old Teresa Broadhurst, who'd just earned her pilot's license in June, took off in the 6-seater plane around midnight and

tried to commit suicide. The paper didn't say that. It very carefully didn't say that. On page 31. In three brief inches. But Broadhurst had the money to buy his way into or out of the news.

The *Times-Gazette* was even more discreet.

PRIVATE PLANE CRASHES

The fact that she'd crashed over water had saved her. It sounded like that had been the only accident. A pilot, taking off with very little fuel, heading north-east over the Atlantic, will not get any place at all except dead.

Keener put the microfilm back in its box and lit another cigarette.

"Library."

"Hi, there, Jimmy. It's Meg. I just wondered if you'd had any thoughts about the heiress."

"Oh. Well now, I did have a couple of names. Got a pencil?"

"Shoot."

"Tiffany Slade. Got it?"

"Mmm."

"Tabatha Cooke. And then I had a genuine piece of inspiration. How about Trish? Now that'd be Patricia, but Trish Huddleston is—"

"Yes. That's possible. Maybe. I don't know exactly what I'm doing. Anything else?"

"Not yet. Will you be wanting the files on these?"

"Yeah. I'll be down to get them right now."

Keener checked the copy of this year's paper for May 17. Page 26. Column 2.

COMMITTEE FOR A BETTER MIAMI
HOLDS GALA

Etcetera. Blah-blah . . . fund-raising dinner . . . ballroom of the Fontainbleau . . . glittering . . . $200-a-plate . . . speakers included . . . the committee's chairman:

> "What Miami really needs in a mayor," Mr. Broadhurst said in his address, "is a man with integrity, commitment, and guts. A young man with good old-fashioned ideas, about law and order, about work and morality. Perhaps a young man such as Harrison Quinn . . ."

Teresa was mentioned in the caption of a picture. She was sitting at a table with U.S. Attorney Harrison Quinn, whose wife was apparently "unable to attend." It was a candid picture. Quinn had been lighting Teresa's cigarette, but what interested Keener was the looks on their faces, the angles of their bodies.

He studied the picture, and then had a photocopy made for his files.

"I'd like to talk to Trish Huddleston, please."

"Who's calling?"

"This is Meg Carter of the *Chronicle-News*."

"Oh. This is she. I was expecting someone to call from the press."

"You were?"

"Montana."

"I beg your pardon?"

"That's the answer to your question."

"Uh, what was the question?"

"Who designed the dress I was wearing last night."

"That wasn't the question."

"It wasn't? I see. Then I guess you want to know what I'll be wearing tonight?"

"No."

"No?"

"What I wanted to talk about is Michael Gallagher."

"I see. . . . Has he done something absolutely smashing?"

"Well, that seems to be the question of the week."

"Oh dear. Just a second. Hold on."

Meg could hear the sound of two women's voices consulting in a low unintelligible buzz.

The phone was picked up again. "I'm a little embarrassed, but let me get this straight. Are you talking about the British shoe designer, or that man in South Africa who's doing such marvelous things with enamel—though Marilyn swears his name's Michael Galopos."

"No. Gallagher. He's not a designer. He's a friend of yours."

"Oh. He is? Oh dear. Well of course I have so many friends I don't really know them all. Can you give me a hint?"

"You were on his boat at the Shoreham last week."

"Oh, no. Not me. The only boat I was on last week was *La Belle Fille de Joie* in St. Tropez. I've been there all summer."

"Oh."

"I got back here yesterday. From Paris, of course, and with the most incredible collection of clothes. What they're doing with shoulders—"

"I'm sorry, Miss Huddleston. Thank you for your time."

Meg put the phone down and looked at the wadded-up pages on the floor. She'd worked all Saturday and Saturday night and now it was Sunday and she still couldn't make up her mind about Gallagher. Every time she tried to write a sentence, she stopped. She believed him; she didn't believe him. She wanted to believe him; she wanted to believe she only wanted the truth. He'd been sly; he'd been honest; he'd been putting her on; he'd been honest even though he'd been putting her on. Her indecision was reflected in her prose.

Mr. Gallagher, reclining on the deck of a boat that was built for the purpose of smuggling whiskey, insisted that he'd never been involved in a crime. "I was smart enough not to," he said with a grin, a smooth kind of grin that made his visitor believe that at least he was smart enough not to admit it.

Asked if he'd ever been involved in a crime, Mr. Gallagher grinned and said earnestly, "No. I was smart enough

Dammit! She looked at the jumble of words. Was he earnest or smooth? Was he lying or not? His blue eyes seemed to be watching her, waiting, asking her, "And who the hell are *you* to be a judge?" And it suddenly occurred to her that that's what she was doing: judging him, not simply writing about him, but passing sentences, instructing a jury of 900,000 (the daily circulation of the *Chronicle-News*) exactly what to think about Michael Gallagher.

And what could she tell them?

And what if she was wrong?

She got up from the desk in the corner of her bedroom and went out to the terrace. Leaning on the railing, she looked at the bay and wondered if Gallagher was out on his boat . . . if the girl whose blue and white suit she'd been wearing was with him . . . if the girl was Nicky or "T."

Everything seemed to be resting on "T."

"T": who knew where he'd been on the tenth; who'd carefully "remembered not to remember." Maybe she knew he'd been kidnapping Diaz. Or maybe she knew he'd been robbing a bank and therefore couldn't have been kidnapping Diaz. Whatever it was, it was something he didn't want known by the Feds. And whatever it was, she'd have to find out. Before she could judge him, before she could write.

The story would just have to wait for the facts.

If McAdam would wait.

He'd have to.

She looked at the clear blue sky and thought about the crazy things that came out of it: Michael Gallagher ...

18.

Monday, it rained.

When Keener arrived, soaking, at nine, at the Federal Building, he was called directly into Shiloh's office, called on the carpet in Shiloh's office. He stood there dripping while Shiloh yelled.

"You know how much fucking *money* that cost?"

Keener nodded.

"Did Rossen tell you to—"

"No. Yes." Keener shook his head. "He told me to at first and I told him I wouldn't. Then I figured I'd better."

"Spend that kind of money?"

"Yeah. Well, I told him you wouldn't go along with it. I said you'd raise hell, and he didn't even argue. Christ." Keener sat. "He knows what he's doing. He gets what he wants and comes out like a rose." Keener laughed.

"I fail to see the humor."

"I know."

Shiloh looked at the overtime sheets. "I just want to understand this. You really think Gallagher's a hot possibility?"

"Hell, I don't even think Rossen really thinks so. The only thing I know is, the minute that goddam leak hit the paper, Gallagher had Malderone's goons on his tail. So what did you want me to do—let 'em kill him? Not that they won't if they want to." He shrugged.

"So you gave him a watchdog. Twenty-four-hour."

"Right."

"For protection, not for surveillance."

"Call it surveillance if it makes you happier."

"Nothing makes me happy. I want you to cancel it."

"Did you talk to Rossen?"

"I don't have to talk to Rossen."

"Because I think he's crazy. I think he's setting up Gallagher as decoy and he wants us to catch some trigger in the act."

"Now *you* sound crazy."

"Yeah. Well."

"I want you to cancel it."

Keener looked at Shiloh, the thin, bespectacled book-keeper's face.

"Quinn doesn't want it," Shiloh went on. "He says it's harassment."

"Quinn wouldn't know his harassment from his elbow. Look: we put Gallagher's life on the line and the least we can do is—"

"Nothing."

"True," Keener said. "That's the least we can do."

Shiloh waved a hand. "I'm sick of hearing about this Gallagher business anyway. What else have you got?"

Keener sneezed and looked at his shoes. They were soaked. Keener blew his nose. "I got a snitch on the street might be close to something."

"What?"

"I don't know. He told me not to call him, so I've got to give him room. He's wired very tight to some pals of Cavaletti. And that's still where my money is. On Cavaletti's goons. I also got a few more—"

"And I got a meeting. We'll talk about it later." Shiloh stood up. "Meanwhile, you'll cancel the baby-sitters, right?"

Keener said nothing.

Shiloh turned and looked sadly out the window. "Jesus. I gotta go out in that shit."

Monday, it poured.

When Gallagher got back from the bank, at eleven, Ortega was pacing the office.

"What now?"

Ortega thumbed at the window. "That."

"They been throwin stones at it?" Gallagher tossed his trenchcoat on a cabinet.

"Mira, mira," Ortega said.

"They been throwin stones at the mira."

"Make jokes."

"No joke. Seven years' bad luck." Gallagher walked over to the back window. A couple of stevedores were sitting in the shed, smoking. One of them was drinking coffee. "Tell me they're taking their coffee break, right?"

Ortega just looked at him.

Muttering, Gallagher settled at his desk, put his feet up. The cuffs of his trousers were wet.

Ortega lit a short French cigarette. "They're takin a wine break." He blew out the match.

"The *Calliope* docked?"

"About an hour ago. With your paid-for wine. The guys start unloading, Rodriguez says stop. He sends a messenger to say it, so Willie says, the hell, if he wants us to stop, then he better come over here and say it himself."

"Willie's okay."

"Means bullshit. Rodriquez is on his way over, and Willie'll walk like the rest of 'em. Got to. If not, he's a scab and they'll cancel his card. No card, he don't work. For no one. They'll knock out a couple of his teeth and then the IDU med fund won't pay to fix em."

"Nice."

"Yeah. It's a nice business. Shit. Always. Jesus. My old man worked on the docks. Back in the thirties. Twelve bucks a week, forty-hour shifts, and if someone dropped a fuckin crate on your back, you came to in the poorhouse with a pinkslip in your hand. Jesus. Ole Hector thought the union was great. Cavaletti was *Dios Segundo,* you know? I don't know. So the prick robbed everybody blind, but the guys did okay. Unless they made waves. Diaz made waves and the waves'll wash him up in Jamaica pretty soon. Half-eaten by sharks." Ortega shook his head. "I don't know, man. I don't know. I mean, for half those guys Cavaletti was God, and for the other half Diaz is Christ of the Andes."

Gallagher looked at him. "What the hell are you talkin about?"

"I'm talkin how they think you did it, man. You crucified Christ. You want to know how long the strike's gonna last? Ask the Jews, man. They been struck now for two thousand years. Here comes Rodriguez. Want to talk to him?"

"I want to punch his face out."

"Yeah." Ortega nodded. "That'll help about as much as talkin to him will."

* * *

On Monday, the tail of the hurricane hit.

When Meg arrived back at the newsroom from lunch, the wind was chasing forty-five miles an hour and depositing a few million inches of water, to the consummate delight of Alonzo Garcia, whose weather report would be a front-page blast.

"Wet enough for ya?" Alonzo said.

Meg dumped her broken umbrella in the basket and peeled off her raincoat. Alonzo stood there.

"Are you waiting for an *answer?*"

"Yeah," Alonzo said. "See, I'm asking that question to see what people say. For a column. I figured it'd be a cute gimmick."

"And what do people say?"

"Nothing," Alonzo said. "Not a damn thing."

Meg poured some coffee and took it to her desk.

McAdam was waiting. "I'm waiting," he said.

She nodded. "I know."

"I don't even know what the hell I'm waiting for. What am I waiting for? What incredible, wonderful, fascinating angle are you working on?"

Meg said nothing.

"Tell me something worth waiting for."

Meg said nothing.

"Meg!"

She looked up. "Mystery Woman."

"Mystery Woman what?"

"Knows where Gallagher was on the tenth."

"Okay. Where was he?"

"I don't know."

"Who is she?"

"I don't know. If I knew that, it wouldn't be a mystery."

McAdam squinted. "Are you making this up?"

"I saw a note in his desk."

"In?"

"In."

McAdam just nodded. "And what did it say?"

She told him.

"And where have you been looking for this dame?"

"In the files. On the phone."

"So how about looking at the Shoreham Marina?"

Meg cocked her head.

McAdam said, "The note was in a desk on his boat. Therefore the woman must have been on his boat and figure maybe somebody there can describe her."

"Oh," Meg said. She glanced out the window and looked at the howling, growling rain. "Jesus. You want me to go out there now?"

Keener's intercom buzzed.

He sneezed into it. "What?"

Donna said, "A Miss Peralta to see you."

"Send her in," Keener said, and stood.

She was wearing a bright yellow slicker and yellow rubber boots and her hair was frizzing out from a soft yellow rainhat. She was holding a yellow umbrella in her hand but she carried it as though it were an M-16.

Keener sneezed again. "Sorry," he said. "Want some coffee?"

"No. I want blood."

He looked at her. "Mine?"

"You got it."

"Yeah. Well, I think you'll have to stand on line." He gestured at a chair. "Want to sit?"

"No."

He shrugged. "Okay." He sat behind his desk. "Shoot. Hold it." He held up his hand. "I don't mean that literally. If you've got a derringer with you, forget it." He sneezed again. "Christ. I don't suppose you'd have any aspirin?"

For an answer, she glared at him. "You're hounding him," she said. "Why do you hate him?"

"Come on, Nicky. I don't even hate my own mother. Why would I hate him?"

"You sent him to jail. I didn't know that before."

"And you don't know it now. Look, I don't like your boyfriend very much, but I thought it was a roust."

"It was."

"I just said so. Go on."

She gave him a quick raking glance. "So you admit you rousted him."

"He socked me. The department pressed charges. I was called to testify. I said if I'd been him I might've done the same thing. You can read it in the transcript. It's public record. And what the hell am I explaining this for? You're right. I rousted him. Go on."

She nodded. "So you're doing it again. This Diaz garbage. You know he didn't do it. Why would he do it? He isn't mixed up with any of those guys. He just minds his own business. Only, if you bastards keep fucking around, he won't have one to mind." Her dark eyes scratched him. "Is that what you're after? Put him out of business?"

Keener said nothing.

"This morning—the bank? They won't give him any loan. They gave him last year, and the year before that. Right out of jail and they gave him. But this year they're giving him bullshit. You know what they said? They said, Listen, you'll be back in jail by the spring. So they won't give him money. And no money means he can't buy liquor, and no liquor means no business."

"I'm sorry," Keener said.

"And then the union struck him. He can't even get the stuff he's already paid for."

Keener said nothing. She stood there, vivid in her anger and her bright yellow coat, and for a moment Keener thought how goddam lucky Gallagher was to have such a fierce and a loyal Nicole. "I'm sorry," he said again.

She grunted. "And a fat lot of good that'll do. How long'll this go on?"

Keener shook his head. "Don't waste your time, Nicky. I can't tell you anything about any investigation in progress."

"But you *could* tell the press."

"It wasn't my office."

"You'd lie if it was."

"Probably. Look, sometimes there are damn good reasons to leak. Only this wasn't one of them. Not from my angle. So I figure your beef is with the leaker and the press. Only you can't come down on the leaker since you don't know who he is, and if you holler at the press they'll just print it that you hollered. So keep on yelling." He looked at his watch. "I got five more minutes."

"You bastard," she said.

He nodded. "Four minutes and fifty-eight seconds."

She opened her mouth again, closed it, turned, and stalked from his office.

He swiveled in his chair and watched her as she went. Her hat flew off and her hair tumbled out.

He sneezed again.

19.

The rain had stopped.

The deck was flooded, but there didn't seem to be any major damage.

Gallagher picked up a bucket. "Jesus. Fire and flood. You remember your Genesis? What comes next?"

"Locusts or boils," Ortega nodded. "Or whales."

"Hey, Mike!" Charlie Wilson was standing on the pier. "Need any help there?"

"Want to grab a bucket?"

"Sure." Charlie came on board, started bailing. After a while he said, "Girl here today. Blonde. She was askin me questions."

"About?"

Charlie shrugged. "About girls. She wanted to know about your girls."

"No shit," Ortega laughed. "You think she wants your body as well as your neck?"

"What did you tell her?"

"Nothin," Charlie said. "Far as I know, you're a Carmelite monk."

Gallagher nodded, continued to bail. "Hey, listen," he said, "if they make a good brandy, I might think it over." He looked at Ortega. "After we finish, I'm buyin you a drink."

"After we finish, I'm goin home to bed."

"You're doin that after I buy you a drink," Gallagher said, "at the R and R Bar."

Ortega looked up in the gilt-framed mirror, put his glass on the bartop, and said, "Pretty cute."

Gallagher looked in the mirror and nodded. Megan Carter had come through the door. She was wearing an open raincoat and, under it, a white silk dress, and on a day when everybody else in the world looked soggy and frizzy and sneezy and glum, the woman looked as fresh as a just-watered daisy. She was heading for a booth. Gallagher nodded. "Yeah. Well, I gotta give her that one. She's cute."

"I mean you, amigo. How'd you know she'd be here?"

"Figured. Bar across the street from the paper? So anyway, I called up Benziger before—I wanted to tell him how the wine'd be late—so I asked him. She's here every night with her friends. Or almost."

"You're crazy."

"Why am I crazy?"

"What do you want with her?"

"Christ. Information."

"That, and what else?"

"Nothing."

"You're crazy."

"Why am I crazy?"

"She burned you before and she'll burn you again."

"Hey, look: she could've blasted me after that boat trip and she didn't."

"There's an old Spanish saying, amigo. 'When your enemy isn't shooting, beware.' "

"Meaning?"

"He's quietly building an A-bomb."

Gallagher nodded. "I can handle her."

"Wrong."

"She's a woman, isn't she?"

"Newspaper woman. A woman made outta newspaper, man. You touch her and you'll just get your hands all dirty."

Gallagher shrugged. "We'll see."

"Not me. First stupid thing I see you do in three years and I don't want to see it." Ortega stood up. "You know what comes after the locusts and the boils?" He stubbed out his cigarette. "The blondes, amigo. The bad-trouble blondes."

She looked up and saw him.

Alicia said, "Isn't that—"

"Yeah. It sure is." Meg studied him, her chin in the cup of her hands. "I ask you, Your Honor, is that the face of a killer?"

"Lady-killer."

"Yeah."

"Want to see me get killed?" Meg picked her drink up.

"You're crazy. He'll kill you."

"But what a way to go."

"You're crazy."

"I want some information."

"On what? The birds and the bees? You're crazy. If he came here, he's after something too."

"I know."

She hesitated, stopping in the middle of the room with a gimlet in her hand and a heart in her throat. But I can handle it, she thought, and she started moving toward him, and wondered if the moth, heading clearly for the candle, had hesitated briefly on the edge of the flame and thought, I can handle it.

He looked at her, registered a flicker of surprise.

"You just happened to be in the neighborhood," she said.

"Maybe. The R and R's one of my customers."

"Oh."

"Disappointed?"

"Try 'disbelieving.'"

He nodded. "Bet you never fell for Santa Claus either."

"Did you?"

"Oh yeah. He's the guy, if you were bad, he gave you some presents. Drink up. I'll buy you dinner." He shrugged. "If you're free."

She sipped at her gimlet. "Another chicken sandwich?"

"Hell no. I'm in a mood to kind of celebrate tonight."

"To celebrate what?"

"Going out of business. The union struck me and the bank turned me down." He grinned.

"Yeah, I get it. That's nice," she said sharply. "So you want me to eat crow. Well forget it, Gallagher. It isn't my fault. I just printed the news."

"Hey, did I accuse you?" He showed her his absolutely innocent hands. "I'm just tellin you more news. I figure I'll probably sell off the warehouse and leave for New York. And you know what's funny? With all this shit going down about Diaz, no one ever told me not to leave town. They do that in the movies, don't they? I mean if they really suspect you?" He lit a cigarette, inspecting her over the dance of the flame. "You want to run away with me to South America?" He clicked off the lighter.

Meg said nothing.

"Hell, in the movies," he said, "you'd say yes."

"What movies you been watchin?"

"Late Show, I guess. I guess they don't make girls like that any more." He shrugged. "Or movies."

She cocked her head at him.

He smiled. "I don't know of any place that serves crow. How about lobster? The Chop House okay?"

"You mean I can walk out anytime I like?"

"Absolutely."

She finished her drink. "So let's go."

In the car, she saw his eyes check the rear-view mirror.

"No photographer," she said.

"Yeah. Just the others."

"What others?"

"Blue Chevy and the black-and-white Ford."

She nodded. "From the same movie, I suppose."

He shrugged, turning into the Chop House parking lot. Neither a Chevy nor a Ford pulled in.

"Nice try," she said sharply.

He ordered champagne. She was starting to enjoy it, the whole absolutely improbable night. They were playing a game, some kind of game, and if she didn't know exactly what the game was, at least she knew it was a game. And she also had the feeling they were equally matched.

He lifted his glass. "To your father," he said. "Hey, we never talked about *your* father, huh? What is he?"

"A Yankee."

"And what does he do?"

"He's a lawyer."

"Well. There's a noble profession. What does he do, work for big corporations?"

"Exactly."

"Corporations are noble too."

She laughed. "You're good, Gallagher. You're really good. You know just how to do it."

"Do what?"

She shrugged. "Whatever you're doing."

Over a two-pound lobster, she tried. "I ran into someone at a party who knows you. I thought she was just
about to sock me." She laughed.

"Yeah? Who was that?"

"Christ, I don't remember. Palm Beach. Rich. Her
name was, uh . . . Damn. All I remember is, uh, something with a T. Tanya. Treva. Uh . . ." Nothing. His
eyes showed nothing at all. She shrugged. "I just thought
you'd like to know you had friends."

"Only friend I got that's a fighter is John. Begins with
a J."

She nodded. "Well, I'm fairly sure this was a girl. So
tell me, Gallagher, you got a lot of girls?"

"You asking that personally, professionally, or what?"

She thought. "Half and half?"

He squinted. "You answered me honestly?"

"Yeah."

He grinned. "Then honestly, no. Just one."

She laughed. "You make it sound as though 'one' is a
lot less serious than ten. It's the other way around, pal."
She finished her wine.

He filled up her glass again and lit a cigarette.

She said, "Do you love this 'one' or just like her?"

He shrugged. "You make it sound as though 'like' is a
lot less serious than love. It's the other way around, pal."
He pinged on his glass. "Did you love your husband?"

"Sure. For a while."

"See what I mean?" He pulled on his cigarette. "I like
Nicky, though. I like her a lot."

"That's nice."

"Uh huh."

"But you aren't in love."

He shook his head slowly. "How about you?"

" 'Love,' you mean? No. I don't want to be either."

"Why not?"

"I don't know. I'm not good at that scene. And I always feel tremendously guilty when it's over. People are
fragile. You drop them, they break."

"And you always think it's 'over'?"

"Isn't it?"

"No. Not for some people. No."

"Yours was."

"Hell. Mine was, I knocked her up so I married her."

"Honorable."

"Yeah. You in love with your job?"

"No. Yes. Well, in a way."

"This Quinn. What's he like?"

"Oh wow!" She cocked her head at him. "And aren't you slick. All that bubbling charm and champagne. That 'are you in love' and you're hustling me. Jesus. And you're not even hustling *me*. Look, I won't tell you the source of that story. I can't and I won't and I won't and I can't. Okay? Understood?"

"Honorable."

"Yeah!" She glared at him.

"So." He was silent for a moment. Shrugging, he looked at her. "Yeah. Okay. Let me try it again. I was at this party and I talked to this fascinating district attorney. Don't remember his name, but it started with a Q." He looked at her levelly.

She lowered her eyes. Pushing her lips out, she nodded. "Got a feeling we've been here before?"

"Yep. Want a brandy?"

"Sure."

He ordered. The waiter called him Mike.

She said, "Is this one of your customers too?"

"Used to be."

"Oh."

"Hey look," he said. "Before, when I asked about Quinn?"

"Yeah?"

"Well, I wasn't even asking whodunit. I just want to know who the ballplayers are. I mean, I figure these honchos in the Justice Department, by now they know more about me than I do. So I just want to hear a little news about them. Your friend Keener, I know."

"Yeah. Well, he isn't as bad as you think he is."

"No? I heard you went out with him."

"Where'd you hear that?"

"I told you. I service the R and R Bar."

"Hold it. You mean the bartender told you?"

He looked at her. "I never reveal my sources."

"That's fair," she said nodding. "That's fair. About Keener: I went out with him once. That's all."

"He in love with you?"

"Keener? Hell, no. He doesn't even like me."

"But you think he isn't bad."

"He's fair and he's honest and he's smarter than I thought he was. Compare him to the rest of those characters up there and he turns out looking like Hopalong Holmes."

"Like what?"

"Like the only white-hat detective."

"What about Rossen?"

"Well, I don't know." She shrugged. "I always cast him as Richard the Third. I think he'd kill babies to get to be king."

"Ambitious."

"Oh yeah. And supposed to be smart. A straight-A brain in a bad-looking body. He looks like a monkey. And Brooks Brothers can't do a damn thing about it. He looks like a monkey in a Brooks Brothers suit. He's scratched his way from Nowhere to Not Far Enough and he absolutely, totally despises Quinn."

"Why?"

"Look at Quinn. Quinn isn't bright. He sailed through Princeton on a stormy C, while Rossen's working nights dishing beans in a hash house and still making Dean's List at N.Y.U. Law. Quinn is a hunk. He's a beefcake beauty and he's married to a page out of *Harper's Bazaar*. Melanie McClintock. Of *the* McClintocks. The big Arizona department store chain. He's social, political, handsome, and rich. He wants to be mayor, and he probably will."

"And why does Rossen hate him?"

"Christ. I just told you."

"Oh yeah." He looked thoughtful, drumming his fingers on the side of his glass. "And wrapping up Diaz would help him be mayor."

"Sure it'd help him. It'd also help Rossen. It'd also help Keener."

"It'd also help me."

"Yeah. If you aren't guilty, it would."

He shook his head slowly. "You still aren't sure."

"No."

"That's nice. That's nice. Do you often have dinner with killers, or what?"

"Mondays. Mondays it's killers. Tuesday it's burglars. Maybe tomorrow I'll have dinner with Ortega. Or was he framed too?"

He stared at her.

"What're you lookin at?"

"You. Your mouth. That's a really big one you got there."

"Yeah? And what're ya gonna do about it, huh?"

His blue eyes studied her. "Something," he said. "Something." He took another sip of his brandy. "Listen," he said, "I don't like what you do, I don't like what you think, but I figure I need you to know me—fast."

"Fine," she said fast. "Get the check and let's go."

Walking through the parking lot, he asked, "Where's your car?" and she told him, at the Press Club.

They drove there in silence. His eyes kept returning to the rear-view mirror and she turned around, peering at the highway behind them, and didn't see the Chevy or the black and white Ford. "You're paranoid," she said.

He was silent.

She was looking at his hand on the wheel. She wanted to touch it. I can handle it, she thought, and smiled, a little dryly, not sure that she could.

His car pulled over to the curb at the Press Club. She turned to him. "So, you're gonna follow me?"

"No. Not tonight."

She felt it like a slap. "You wanted me to know you fast, you said."

He shrugged. "Yeah. So maybe what I meant there was 'well.'"

"If you're not interested," she said, "just say so."

He looked at her; he didn't say a goddam word. But she hadn't just imagined that he'd wanted her. It was there. Or it had been.

"Look, I'm twenty-seven. I don't need the courting."

He shrugged. "I'm forty-seven," he said. "I guess I do."

She felt herself flushing and she opened the door angrily and got out quickly, then turned. "If you're trying to make me feel cheap—" she said.

"Yeah?"

"You're succeeding." She slammed the door, *bang!* in his face.

20.

Something was wrong.

Ortega's little Pacer was parked in the driveway with its door wide open. And every single light in the house was turned on.

Gallagher yelled. "Johnny?"

Nothing.

The door to the house was just slightly ajar.

He took a combat crouch and then pushed the door open.

Nothing flew out.

No bullet.

No fist.

He edged his way in.

The house was a shambles. Understatement. The Rose Bowl game had been played in this house and both sides had lost.

He moved through the wreckage. "Johnny?"

Nothing.

He got to the kitchen.

His stomach turned over. Ortega was lying very still on the floor. They'd done a good job on him. Most of his face was swollen and raw. There were purplish bruises and drying blood.

He was breathing.

Gallagher knelt on the floor. "Hey, Cisco," he whispered.

An eyelid fluttered. The mouth opened slightly, then closed. The other eyelid opened, a slit.

"I got terrible news for you," Gallagher said. "You're gonna live."

Ortega was lying on the bed. He had sixteen stitches in the side of his face. The doctor had left.

Gallagher was sitting in a rocker by the window. "Want to talk for a little?"

Ortega nodded.

"Which army was it?"

Ortega mumbled.

"Can't hear you. You just want to sleep for a while?"

"Salvation . . ."

"What?"

"Salvation Army. Two little old guys. Hit me with a . . ."

"What?"

"Prayerbook."

"Terrific. Repeat: who?"

"I dunno, man . . . linebackers . . . two of 'em . . . jumped me. They . . ."

"What?"

Ortega smiled crookedly. "They musta thought I was you."

"They were waiting in the house?"

Ortega nodded. "Nicky . . ."

"Aw, Jesus. What?"

Ortega held up a hand. "S'all right. . . . Called me. Came over here. House really fucked."

"Nicky came over here?"

Ortega nodded.

Gallagher thought. "She came to the house and it was already done, so she called you and left."

"Left, then called."

"So then you came over, walked into the house, and they—"

"Jumped me."

"Describe them."

"Forty-six guys. Twenty-seven feet tall."

"Cisco . . ."

"I put up . . . hell of a fight. One of 'em's prob'ly got a . . ."

"What?"

"Sore fist."

"Christ." Gallagher laughed.

"Broken nose. No shit."

"Describe them."

"Blonde . . . ape. . . . Other one . . . dark. Dark one had a scar on his . . . *big* scar . . ."

"On his hand. And he used brass knuckles."

Ortega nodded.

"Six-two, dark-haired, ugly as a waterbug."

"Yeah."

"Spungeilli."

"You know him?"

"Kind of. I know who he is. Rest now, buddy."

"Hello?"

"Miss Lovett? I'm terribly sorry to disturb you at night. This is Megan Carter."

"Yes, Miss Carter?"

"I, uh, we work for the same paper."

"We do?"

"You *are* the society editor?"

"Of course, dear. And what, may I ask, are you?"

"I cover the federal courts and agencies."

"Oh. That doesn't sound amusing at all. Is it?"

"It isn't even trying to be."

"Well, if you're looking for a job on Society——"

"No. I just wanted a little information. I was told you know everything about everyone in Miami, and I——"

"Not in Miami, dear. Palm Beach, definitely. Miami Beach, regrettably. But goodness—*Miami?*"

"Well, anyway, it's Palm Beach I'm interested in. Specifically heiresses. Specifically an heiress whose name begins with *T.*"

"Oh. I see. Are we playing a guessing game, dear? Some chic new party game imported from, perhaps, Boise?"

"No. I need some information. Do you know any heiress whose name begins with *T* who might be connected to Michael Gallagher?"

"*The* Michael Gallagher?"

"Yes."

"Now *there* is a beautiful boy. My, my. What bones. His father was a devastating devil of man. A scoundrel, of course. Let me think for a minute. What Palm Beach heiress whose name begins with T is connected to . . . No. I give up, dear. Who?"

"That was my question."

"Oh. Well, let me think again. Andrea Thomas. No. She's too old, but perhaps—"

"It's the first name that starts with a T."

"Well, goodness. Why didn't you say so, dear. That's Teresa Broadhurst."

21.

Malderone's house was a cream-colored stucco with a red tile roof and a riot of clashing bougainvillea on the walls, a Spanish style mansion built in the thirties with a kidney-shaped pool and a six-car garage.

A butler showed Gallagher into a study where a muscle squad jumped him, slammed him on the wall, frisked him, abruptly spun him around, opened his shirt, and then, shrugging, smiled.

"Sorry there, Mike, but you coulda been wired."

"Miked," said the other one. "Mike could be miked." He laughed like the idiot he probably was.

Gallagher nodded and buttoned his shirt, looking from one goon's face to the other. The last time he'd seen them they'd been crashing a Buick, but they didn't really seem to be holding any grudge.

The butler returned and showed him out to the pool, where Malderone was having a leisurely breakfast at a wrought-iron table. He was wearing a navy blue terry cloth robe, and his hair had been dyed to an odd blue-black that practically matched it. He was trim. He looked up from a plateful of yogurt and nodded. "So," he said. "The mountain comes."

Gallagher shrugged and sighed. "I didn't seem to have very much choice."

Malderone lidded his eyes as in pain. "Is that how you talk to me, Michael?" he said. "With so little respect? Have I not respected your wishes, Michael?" He put down his spoon and shook his head sadly. "People ask me about you. They wonder how you are. They wonder why you aren't here for Christmas dinner."

"Yeah. Well." Gallagher sat. "And then some of them know exactly how I am. And exactly where. How come your muscles've been tailing me, Santos?"

"Ah! Coffee, Michael?"

"No. Thanks."

Malderone picked up a large silver pot. "After the mornings now, I can't drink the coffee. Even one little cup at dinner—one cup—and I'm watching the dawn." He sighed heavily, filling his cup. "Life shows us pleasures and snatches them away. Time is a thief, Michael."

"Yeah. Why the tail?"

Malderone shrugged. From his pocket he pulled out a small silver clipper and started to manicure a ten-buck cigar. "I read of your recent problems in the paper. I sent a few friends to offer my help." He lit the cigar and then puffed on it quickly till he had the thing drawing just the way he liked it. "Your refusal of the offer was, shall we say, emphatic. The Buick cost fifteen hundred to repair."

"I didn't know it was yours."

"But you figured it out."

"Later. I recognized the guys in the Chevy."

"And you still didn't come to me. You still didn't come to me. You still didn't come to me and say, Uncle Santos, I'm in trouble. Help me. Advise me. This"—Malderone blew a perfect smoke ring— "this caused me certain serious concerns. It acted like a cup of espresso after dinner. I tossed. I turned. I wondered: is Michael making deals with the state?"

"No."

"Does Michael intend to?"

"No. I got nothing to deal about."

"True? You know nothing?"

"Nothing."

"Maybe. Maybe. So far. Still, perhaps you could try to find out."

"It's none of my business."

"They could make it your business. If they push you hard enough, you might help them out. You know a lot of people. You could start asking questions."

"Is that why you're tailing me?"

Malderone said nothing. He smoked his cigar. His hooded eyes blinked in the sun like a lizard's.

"Spungeilli paid me a visit."

"I heard. Regrettable. Sad. Sad. But you can't have it both ways, Michael. Certain people felt you weren't, shall we say, completely reliable. Since you hadn't come to see me, I couldn't, in conscience, offer reassurance. I'm sure you can see that."

"They beat up a friend of mine."

Malderone shrugged. "He was just another piece of furniture, Michael. It was meant as a part of the warning to you. Believe me, to prevent it was beyond my control. Spungeilli works for . . . others."

"Yeah. I know."

"No. You don't know. The fact of Spungeilli tells you nothing at all. If you pursued it, I would send many flowers to your funeral and think you were a fool. I offer you that." Malderone moved his chair back to follow the fast-moving slant of the sun. "As my nephew, of course, I would offer you more. I would offer to repair any damage inflicted by the government's actions. To your business, for instance."

"That's an offer I'd refuse."

"Yes."

"Thanks anyway."

Malderone shrugged. "Of course there are those who'd make you offers you couldn't."

"Am I being set up?"

Malderone turned his head. "By who?"

"I don't know. Maybe someone you know."

"You're my nephew."

"Yeah. Well. Maybe someone who knows I'm not here for Christmas dinner."

"Even so. In whose interest would it possibly be?"

"Someone who wants to take the heat off himself?"

"For what? For a couple of days? For a week? No. If they wanted to frame you, Michael, you'd be framed. There'd be bloodstains drying in the trunk of your car. There'd be witnesses telling how they saw you at the beach. Even then, if you could prove where you were on the tenth— Can you?"

"Yeah. If it's that or Death Row."

"So. There you are! No. You're looking on the wrong side of the law. Your answer's on the other side. They're setting you up to play pigeon, that's all."

Gallagher thought about the pigeon, dead and bloody and hung by a rope from the door of his garage. "I won't," he said slowly.

"Alas, a lot of people seem to think that you will."

"A lot of people?"

"Counting both sides of the street. One side hopes, the other side fears. That puts you with both sides aiming at the middle."

"And the middle is me."

Malderone nodded. "The man in the middle."

"Lucky Pierre."

"So what will you do, Michael?"

Gallagher thought. "Christ. I don't know. I don't know. What Tommy would have done, I guess. Wait." He shrugged. "And then punt."

Malderone smiled. "You're very much like him, you know? A lot more like him than you think you are."

"No." Gallagher looked at the platinum blonde in the yellow bikini coming out of the house. "No. But I guess I know how to be," he said.

"Miss Broadhurst?"

"Yes."

"This is Megan Carter. From—"

"I know what you're from. Transylvania."

"Oh. Well, I'm sorry you feel that way. Because I'm working very hard to try and clear Michael Gallagher. And I think you could help me."

There was silence.

"You could help *him*, is what I mean. I think you could clear him. Would you talk to me?"

Silence.

"Miss Broadhurst, as his friend, why won't you help him?"

Silence.

"Miss Broadhurst?"

"I'll be at my studio at four this afternoon. No. I don't want to be seen with you. I'll be . . . I'll be at Vizcaya. In the garden. At four."

"How will I know you?"

"I'll know you."

Keener blew his nose. His cold, like a nasty poisonous fruit, had ripened overnight. It was a peach. He was

drinking tea instead of coffee, at Donna's suggestion, and
he sneezed directly at his morning tea.

Hamilton came in and said, "Germ warfare. We could
ship you to Russia, we could end the cold war."

"Cute," Keener said. He blew his nose again and lit a
cigarette. "Got another phonecall from our friend this
morning."

"Which friend?" Hamilton said. "We got so many."

"Ross. Remember Ross?"

"The upstanding neighbor."

Keener nodded dryly. "Trustworthy type."

"Yeah. There's a guy who calls a spic a spade. Bet he's
voting for Quinn. What's he telling us this time?"

"Something. Gallagher was blitzed last night."

"Drunk?"

"Blitzed. As in the London blitz. Three goons went
through his house like a white tornado."

"Was Gallagher hit?"

"Nope. Wasn't there. Ortega was, though."

"Did Ross call the cops?"

"You kidding? He watched it like the nine o'clock
movie. Why he called me was, I'd showed him a picture
of Spungeilli last week."

"Spungeilli was one of them?"

Keener nodded. "Got a date on tonight?"

Hamilton finished a bad-looking danish. He licked his
fingers. "Yeah."

"Cancel it. You and me are gonna lock up the barn."

"Gonna what?"

"The horse got stolen last night. No stakeout last night.
So we're gonna work a little bit of unpaid overtime. Also
get Golden and Block to volunteer. Christ. Would I have
loved to get ahold of Spungeilli. In the act." He sneezed
again.

Hamilton said, "Nothing personal, buddy, but I don't
want to sit in a car with you tonight. I'll get Golden,
okay?"

"Golden boy won't want to sit with me either."

"I'll go with Golden. You go with God."

"Maybe. We'll see."

"Why'd they hit him?"

Keener shrugged. "But it's sure as hell bringing them

out of the woodwork, isn't it. Jesus. What a total fuckup. Rossen starts a fire and Shiloh starts firing the firemen. Shit."

Donna walked in and deposited a pile of papers on his desk. "I tried to get that number in Jacksonville again. No luck."

"Keep trying."

She nodded. "Can I get you another cup of tea?"

Keener looked at her. "What happened to Liberation?"

"We voted to suspend it during illness," she said. "You look like you're dying."

"Thanks," Keener said. "Just keep trying the Jacksonville call."

"So what's in Jacksonville?" Hamilton said.

"A longshot." Keener looked at his sneezed-on tea. He shrugged, then drank it.

22.

Vizcaya was a thirty-acre estate, according to the glossy color brochure, and the mansion, an elaborate Venetian palazzo, had seventy rooms filled with art and antiques, open to the public from nine to five daily, tickets $2.50, students and military personnel $1, children 50¢.

Meg dropped the booklet and looked at her watch. 4:25. She was being stood up, literally led down the garden path. She paced around the base of a tiered coral fountain surrounded by flowers and shaded by palms, and sat on the edge of it, idly dipping her fingers in the pool.

A voice said, "Well. Michael said you were pretty."

Meg looked up. Teresa Broadhurst was tall and dark, with heavy, exotically frizzed-out hair and eyes that were a startling emerald green. She was wearing a midi-length cowgirl skirt, an elaborately embroidered Mexican shirt, and a big straw hat. Lifting her shoulders, she added, "But definitely not his type." Delivering that one, she tossed back her head, a gesture that was either nervy or nervous, like a horse that was just about to rear or to bolt, and then sat on the edge of the fountain near Meg. "What do you want?"

And Meg let her have it: "I want to know where Gallagher was on the tenth, and I know you remember."

For a moment the woman went totally pale and Meg almost paled, thinking, My God, he did it and she knows. Abruptly, she lifted her big straw bag and Meg thought, she's leaving, she'll get up and walk. Instead she fumbled through the clutter for a while till she pulled out a package of More cigarettes. They were long and brown and looked like delicate, skinny cigars. "Want one?" she asked.

"No," Meg said. "I'm trying to quit."

"And I bet you're the type who's succeeding."

"Yes."

A Dupont lighter clicked out a flame. Broadhurst took a long, slow drag of her smoke. Her hand was shaking. "Michael wasn't here on the tenth," she said tightly. "He wasn't in Miami."

"Were you with him?"

"Yes."

"Where?"

"That's irrelevant."

"Hardly."

Broadhurst was silent, smoking; her eyes seemed focused on the faraway air.

"Look," Meg said. "I have to have a little harder information than the fact that one of his girlfriends—"

"You think I'm his girlfriend."

"One of them, I said."

"Meow, you said. You got a thing for him, Carter?"

"No! I just want to get the facts."

"I see." Teresa Broadhurst laughed, nervously. "Well, the fact is we're very good friends. That's all."

"If you were really such 'very good friends,' you'd want to help him, and to help him you'll just have to tell me where—"

"I can't!" The green eyes were suddenly pleading. "Oh my God, don't you think I'd tell you if I could? I can tell you he's innocent. I can tell you that. But I can't let you print that I'm the one who told you. Don't ask me to do that."

"Then you're no friend at all. What the hell can I print? 'Michael Gallagher is innocent, according to a totally anonymous source who won't back it up'?"

"*Because I can't!*" Teresa Broadhurst stood, started pacing. "You don't know the kind of trouble I'd be in if I did."

"From the mob?"

She laughed hysterically. "Worse. From my father."

"From your father?" Meg looked at her incredulously. "Come on. You look like a big girl to me. What'll he do? Spank you? Send you to bed without supper? I have to have something provable to print."

Teresa Broadhurst stared at her, wide-eyed, thinking. Her hand was shaking again. She fumbled in her bag, pulled out a pillbox with light blue pills, and swallowed one, raw. She continued pacing, silent, pale in the sunlight. Finally she said, "If I told you, if I told you exactly where we were and it cleared him, would you have to put my name in the paper?"

"Probably."

"Why? You printed the first time without any names. 'Knowledgeable sources.' So why couldn't *I* be a knowledgeable source?"

"Because the first time I knew the source was reliable. I believed him."

"And you're saying you don't believe me."

"I've never met you before, and you're a friend of his, which gives you a motive to be lying."

"And his enemies couldn't have a motive?" she said. "Never mind." She shook her head quickly. "Never mind. If I give you the facts you can check them. And you won't have to bother with my name."

"I don't know," Meg said. "First I'd have to hear what the facts really are. Then I'd have to check with my editor."

"You would?" The green eyes widened, mocking. "Come on. You look like a big girl to me. What's the matter? Scared of an editor?"

"No. But there are rules."

"The Golden Rule not being one of them."

"Look, I'm a reporter. You're talking to a newspaper now, not a Sunday school class. Do you understand that? And before we can talk about what I would print, first I have to know if there's a story there at all."

Teresa Broadhurst was silent again. Her hand kept shaking. She looked like a highly unreliable source—except for the fact that her hand kept shaking. Her fear was real, therefore the story she was frightened to talk about was probably real.

"I'll tell you," she said vaguely, "and you'll see—you'll have to see that it's—" She stopped and was silent. Moments went by. On the path by the fountain a four-year-old kid tripped on the gravel and started to cry. His mother picked him up, kissing his knee.

"I had a stupid affair."

Meg turned. "With Michael?"

"No! It was Michael who told me it was stupid. He was

right. I was falling in love with the man. It was stupid. He was married. And I am a big girl and I should have known better. I guess I was . . . I told Michael I was desperately in love and Michael said, no, you're just desperate." She laughed. "And then I was desperately pregnant, and the man had said he didn't want to see my anymore and I, uh, I went to see Michael and Michael wasn't there, and I waited for hours and I, uh . . ." She stopped talking; she looked about to cry.

"Miss Broadhurst," Meg said, "what about the tenth?"

Broadhurst said angrily, "I had an abortion on the tenth, all right? I found out the name of a doctor in Atlanta and Michael went with me. He was with me all the time. Every second, every minute, every day of that weekend. All right?"

Meg nodded. "All right," she said calmly. "I really don't see what you're terrified about. So you had an abortion. It's the nineteen-eighties."

"Not in *my* house, it isn't. It's the nineteen-fifties. Or the eighteen-nineties. And my father'll be—Jesus, he's Franklyn Broadhurst! Do you know what that means? He's a goddam Moral Majority of one. You *can't* print that story."

Meg shook her head. "I told you, Miss Broadhurst, it's not up to me. It's my editor. But listen, you'll be helping Michael. Isn't that what's important? He's in trouble and you're helping him by telling me the truth. I even bet your father'll admire you for that. Listen, did you keep any records of the trip? Hotel bills, ticket stubs? Teresa?"

Teresa Broadhurst was staring, just staring with her big, green, almond-shaped eyes. She stood, still staring wildly at Meg, and then bolted, running quickly away down the path.

"Where are you calling from?" Hamilton said.

"Beach."

"You're lying in the sun while I'm breaking my balls?"

"It's cloudy," Keener said. "And you got more balls than you know what to do with. You wanted to talk to me."

"Yeah. I was down at the Marina again. I got witnesses

telling me Teresa Broadhurst was on Gallagher's boat the
afternoon of the fire."

"The fire was at night."

"Yeah. And I'm not even sure it was Broadhurst. But
it sounds like her, though. She got there at four, was still
there at seven. Nobody knows exactly when she left, but
she was gone before the fire. What's up at the beach?"

"Prices," Keener said. "A one-bedroom condo is a half-
million bucks."

"Thinking of taking one?"

"Two," Keener said. "They're small."

Meg sat drinking coffee at her desk, her mind project-
ing pictures on the blank gray screen of the Display-
writer: Gallagher, lighting a cigarette ("You want to run
away with me to South America?"); Teresa Broadhurst,
running down the path. Gallagher, sitting in the Chop
House Restaurant, watching her with solemn sea-blue
eyes, shaking his head at her ("You still aren't sure?").

She was sure. She started typing; the words appeared
instantly, flashing on the screen.

A 34-year-old Palm Beach woman, daughter of
one of the area's leading citizens, said late Tuesday
she could prove Michael Gallagher was not in Miami
on the day Joseph Diaz

"Aw shit," McAdam muttered. "So what the hell's
that?"

She turned and looked up at him. "The story?" she
said.

"What story? That's not a story, that's a yawn.
C'mere." He started typing in a rapid hunt-and-peck.

Teresa Broadhurst, daughter of Franklyn Broadhurst, a leading proponent of the Right to Life move-
ment, stated late Tuesday she was with Michael
Gallagher "every second" of the day on which Joseph Diaz disappeared. Gallagher, she told the
Chronicle-News in an exclusive interview, got her an
abortion in

*   *   *

"Now *that,*" McAdam said, leaning back, "is a story."

Keener read the instructions on the back of the box of Lipton Noodle Soup (with Real Chicken Broth).

Boil 4 cups of water in a medium saucepan.

He wasn't sure what a medium saucepan was. He had a pan that was big enough to boil two eggs, and another one he made spaghetti in. He filled the spaghetti pot with water and stood there, in defiance of popular wisdom, waiting till it boiled.

Teresa Abigail Broadhurst, he thought. Jesus. The story was political dynamite, and what in the hell should he do about it? Nothing, he decided. Type up the interviews and lock them in a drawer. Before Rossen got ahold of them. Rossen would use them—for sheer, personal, political spite. There was nothing in the story that related to Gallagher. At least not yet.

Reduce heat and stir in contents of one envelope of soup mix. Simmer 5 minutes, stirring occasionally.

He dumped in the soup mix and to hell with the stirring.

He changed into a bathrobe, stuffing the pockets with a big wad of Kleenex, and sprawled on the sofa. He picked up a copy of the *Chronicle-News:* "8 PM: LOBO (Rerun)"

Jesus. Christ. He hurled the paper at the television set. His life, he decided, was becoming a rerun. Boredom, repeated. Mickey Mouse news. He picked up the pocket-size Sony recorder and reran the interview with Alan Demarco of Demarco Galleries, where Broadhurst had once shown her paintings last year. The man was a fountain, didn't need to be pumped; he'd just kept bubbling, shooting off his mouth, dancing all around his sculptures and blatting. "Oh my *dear,*" he'd kept saying.

"Neurotic? Oh my *dear.* She's been in and out of Cloverdale seventeen times. I exaggerate. Five. She's got a whacked-out vision but it works into something quite visually wonderful. Weird, but wonderful. She even got quite a few wonderful reviews. Now picture this, imagine this, Broadhurst himself comes down to the exhibit, and he looks at the paintings, and, my dear, he wants to have her committed on the spot, and he says to her—I swear this on seventeen Bibles—he hollers at her, 'Can't you do *anything* normal?' I suppose it isn't funny. I mean, there she is—Terry—the living skeleton in Franklyn's closet, and I think he wants to lock her in the closet for good. He had her *doctor* come down here to look at the paintings— to *diagnose* the paintings. Can you feature that? Oh my *dear,* what a scene. And the poor thing's terrified. Absolutely cowed. I mean, all he has to do is sign a little piece of paper and she's back in the hatch with some weird Doctor Greeble putting *jolts* in her brain. Her hand shakes so much after that, she can't paint . . ."

Keener clicked off the Sony and looked at his watch.

"I don't know." Meg looked at the words on the screen. "I mean, isn't the point that she was with him that day? I mean, Mac, are you sure we have to mention the abortion?"

McAdam just stared at her. "Hey, are you crazy? It's the only thing that makes me believe that story. In fact, the abortion's the only story there."

"What the hell do you mean, it's the only story there? If—"

"You ever read the paper? Broadhurst was speaking at a dinner last week. Quote: 'Women who have abortions should be locked up for murder.' Unquote. Are you telling me it isn't a story?"

"Oh." Meg was silent. Still, she thought quickly, nothing really terrible could happen to Teresa. Franklyn Broadhurst couldn't lock her up for murder, but someone could try to lock Gallagher up. "But the important thing is it'll clear Gallagher."

"Clear him? You honestly think it'll clear him?"

"I broke my tail to get a hold of that story."

"To clear him?" McAdam cocked his head at her. "Dumb, Meg. Dumb. If he's involved in it, the smartest place to be was out of town. You know what a triggerman is? A hit man? A contract killer? He's hired to do the kill-

ing while the boss is out of town. Come on. Wrap it up. I
want to make the first edition."

"You're wrong, Mac. Michael didn't hire any killer,
and the story's gonna help him."

" 'Michael'?" McAdam lifted his brows. "I see." He
nodded. "I see, I see. Are you writing a news story here
or a love story, huh?"

But before she could answer, he'd turned and walked
off.

The soup was boiling. It smelled pretty good. Keener
poured it into a cereal bowl and then looked for the
chicken. No chicken. There used to be some little chunks
of chicken in the soup, he was practically sure of it; but
possibly not. He blew his nose loudly and returned to the
sofa, inhaling the steam from the chickenless soup. The
steam made him cough, and the soup spilled over on a
page of his notes—right between the lines, where it said
that Teresa had been sleeping with Quinn.

A couple of doormen at the Diplomat condo, where
Quinn kept a studio, had easily identified Teresa from her
picture. She'd been there in the spring, quite often, they
said.

What interested Keener was the question of why. Why
would Quinn be playing with that kind of fire?

Maybe exactly because it was fire. Rebellion. Revenge.
His nature's way of saying fuck you to Franklyn. Politi-
cally Quinn was in bed with the Committee for a Better
Miami, and he really didn't like it. He had just enough
honor to feel a twinge of conscience.

A prick of conscience. That was Harrison Quinn.

And anyway, Terry was a good-looking dame.

Who also had a penchant for playing with fire.

On planes.

On boats?

He'd find out in the morning. He'd visit the lady the
first thing tomorrow, and maybe he could wrap up the
Gallagher angle: fire, gun, D-day, and all.

He finished the soup and then, sighing, recovered the
Chronicle-News: "9 PM: (TV MOVIE) 'Wings of
Death.' Town invaded by killer bats."

This time he hurled the paper at the wall.

23.

The first edition came out at 9:45. The papers were delivered to the R & R Bar, and Meg grabbed a copy on her way out the door.

McAdam had done it. Sixty-point type.

TERESA BROADHURST'S
ATLANTA ABORTION:
GALLAGHER'S ALIBI?
(Story, page 3)

She rushed to the phonebooth and tried to call Michael. There hadn't been an answer when she'd tried him before. This time there was.

Nicole Peralta answered his phone.

Meg hung up.

Quinn spilled coffee on the linen tablecloth.

Melanie said, "You're a slob, you know? At heart, you're a slob. You know that?" She said it very cheerfully though.

Quinn just nodded, holding his breath.

(Story, page 3)

He turned to page 3 and skimmed it. He didn't see his name on the page. His eyes moved quickly till they hit on the sentence "While Broadhurst denies that the child was Gallagher's . . ." The sentence implied that it probably was.

Quinn let his breath out slowly. He smiled. "We got another English muffin?" he asked.

Nicky said, "Is it?"

"Is it true?"

"Is it yours."

"No. My God. What difference would it make?" Gallagher picked up the phone again, dialed. There was still no answer. He reached for his shirt.

"Will it help you?" Nicky said.

"I didn't need that kind of help." He yanked on his jeans. "I haven't killed anybody." He grabbed for his wallet as he stepped into shoes. "Yet."

Palm Beach was a full hour's drive from Miami. It was better to call and try to make an appointment than to waste two hours on a goose chase.

"Broadhurst residence."

"This is Robert Keener of the FBI. Is Miss Broadhurst there?"

"Uh, hold on, please." The butler dropped the phone with a noisy clank that made Keener wince. This morning the cold had settled in his ears. He looked at the clock. It was ten after eight.

"This is Franklyn Broadhurst and the story in the paper is completely untrue. This phone has been ringing off the hook this morning and I won't—"

"I can imagine," Keener said quickly, and wondered what the hell was in the paper this morning. "I'd just like to talk to Teresa. I'm sure if I do, we can straighten this out."

Silence.

"She isn't here. Didn't sleep here. She might be at her studio. At any rate, she isn't answering the phone. But I can tell you, she hasn't seen Gallagher in years."

"Yeah. Well, I'm sure you're right," Keener said, and added, for the hell of it, "Have a nice day."

On his way to the studio he bought the late edition of the *Chronicle-News,* so he wasn't too surprised when there wasn't any answer to his knock on her door. He jiggled the doorknob and found himself surprised when it didn't resist.

He entered the studio.

It seemed to be empty and it seemed to be in order—a large, sunny room with its one glass wall facing out on a garden. When he'd been here before he hadn't studied the paintings; he looked at them briefly. "Weird and wonderful," Demarco had said. Well, they were weird. Large

abstractions in primary colors. An unfinished canvas
rested on an easel. He probed it with a finger. The paint
was still wet. In a smaller window, over on the right, a
loud air conditioner rattled and chugged. She might have
left it on to help the paint dry faster. Still . . . something
bothered him. He looked around again. There was the
same coffee table and the studio couch where she'd sat
and talked with him the first time he'd been here. No sign
that anyone had slept on the couch. On the floor, beside
it, half underneath it, was a newspaper. Keener bent over,
picked it up. The *Chronicle-News*. He looked at the mast-
head: the first edition. She'd bought it last night.

There was a firmly closed door on the wall beside the
couch. Keener looked at it, hating it; not dreading it, just
hating it.

Gallagher saw the ambulance at the curb, the cop-cars
with their flashing, revolving red lights. He hesitated,
stopping his car in the middle of the street. A cop waved
him on, "No loitering, buddy." Keener was walking down
the red brick path. He came over to the window of Gallagher's car and just stood there; he shook his head slowly.

Gallagher closed his eyes. "When?"

"Last night."

He felt the lousy sting of the tears.

"I think we'd better talk," Keener said. "Not here."

"Not now."

Keener nodded. "Get lost," he said. "Go on your boat
and get lost. Just be back by tomorrow."

"Meg?" McAdam's voice had a sonorous ring.

She looked up at him. "My God," she said, "what's
wrong with *you?*" She noticed the city room was eerily
quiet. People were looking at her. "What happened?" she
said.

McAdam shifted his weight, shrugging uneasily. "Accident," he said.

She waited. "Did somebody blow up my car?"

"Teresa Broadhurst. She . . . she killed herself," he said
in a burst.

"How?"

"Slit her wrists. Keener found her in a bathtub."

"She leave any note?"

"No. I don't think so." McAdam was watching her. "Meg . . . ?"

"Do you want me to cover it or what?"

"No," McAdam said. "No. I'll have somebody else do it."

"Oh."

"Do you want to go home?"

"No. Of course not."

"Are you feeling okay?"

"No. I don't think so. No, I feel numb. I can't feel anything." She laughed harshly. "I can't feel my toes, doc. Think I'll ever dance the fandango again?"

"It isn't your fault."

"Sure it isn't, Mac. The only thing I did was to track the woman down and then get her to tell me what she didn't want to tell—and then I didn't listen to her. No. I feel swell."

McAdam shook his head at her. "I want you to remember this. I want you to pay attention. The woman had a psychiatric history. She was unstable."

Meg nodded slowly. "And I should have seen that."

"How could you see that?" He frowned. "And look, it was my decision to publish the abortion—"

"And you don't feel bad."

"Sure, I feel bad. But I'm not blaming myself. Things happen, that's all. People get caught in the middle of things. Listen, remember a year ago when someone tried to shoot the governor and some guy in the crowd grabbed the gun away? Hero. Then it turned out he'd been in jail as a rapist, and the next day the country knew that about him, too."

"Did he kill himself?" Meg said bitterly.

"Hey, look," McAdam said. "Just . . . Let me take you home. It isn't your fault, Meg."

She nodded at him slowly, through tears. "Then why," she said, "do I have to go home?"

She was waiting on his boat when he got there. His first impulse was to pick her up bodily and toss her into the water. The trouble was, the water wasn't deep enough.

"Get out of there," he said.

She didn't move. She just leaned on the rail, looking ravaged. "I can't," she said finally.

"I'm warning you."

He watched her. She still didn't move. He jumped to the deck.

She said, "Michael," and started moving toward him. "Oh, Michael. Please. I just want you to—"

He slammed her back against the rail and then pinned her there. "You just want what?" he said. "A story?" He looked at the glitter of fear in her eyes. "Or you think I'm gonna let you off easy and kill you? Forget it, lady. Christ," he let go of her, "I bet you bleed ink. I bet if you slashed your wrists you'd bleed ink."

"Michael," she said, and he couldn't stand the sound of her.

"Shut it!" He covered her mouth with his hand. "Just shut it, just shut it. You threw someone's life away. Jesus, for what? For something people wrap their garbage in tomorrow. Only yours comes with garbage already in it. Jesus, you're a cool, self-satisfied bitch." She moaned against his hand and he only pressed it harder. "I don't want to hear. I don't want to hear your little stupid excuses. You're inexcusable. What did you do to her? She was so damn scared. She was right on the edge and you pushed her, you pushed her. My God, are you blind? Couldn't you see it? Or you saw it and you didn't give a damn, right?"

Again she tried to move. Again he held her tighter and pressed her to the rail. "There was a kid in New York who got stripped, he got stripped naked in the streets by a mugger and then he got chased by a crowd and he killed himself. You understand? You understand that? You know what it's like? To be naked? To be stripped naked for a crowd?" He ripped at her blouse. It opened and her hands moved instinctively to close it. "Oh no you don't!" He pinned her arms behind her back and then ripped off her blouse. It dangled at her waist. She tried to run, but he grabbed her, spinning her around, yanking at the cord of a wrap-around skirt that came away in his hand, and she stood there, braless and barechested, wearing only black bikini pants, and a crowd started gathering. "You like it?" he said. "You like it? That's what you do every day. You strip people naked and throw 'em to the crowd."

This time she bolted and ran down below.

"Show's over," he yelled at the crowd. "All done."

When he got to the cabin he found her on the bed, sitting, her knees hugged tight to her chest. Her eyes looked glassy.

"It was Rossen," she said. "Elliot Rossen leaked that story about you. I don't know why."

He nodded, tossing the skirt at her. "Here." He grabbed an old sweater of Nicky's from the closet and threw it on the bed. He glanced at her, once. She looked small and frightened, and he didn't feel exactly good about it either. He moved toward the hatch. "Get dressed, and get out."

"Game's over, Elliot."

Rossen plucked a red rubber band from his pocket and aimed it at the lampshade. "Not till I say."

"Delta Airlines says. The Fairmount Hotel says. Mr. and Mrs. Michael Gallagher checked in the night of August the ninth and checked out on the twelfth. Paid by American Express. His signature. Five room-service tabs on Friday the tenth; his signature. The Atlanta office showed his picture to the desk clerk and the room-service waiter. You want to hear more?"

"I don't need to hear more. So he didn't pull the trigger, that's all. Cavaletti has an alibi. Malderone has an alibi. So does Gallagher. So?"

"He isn't in with those guys and you know it."

"Do I? Then how come Spungeilli's tearing up his house?"

"Exactly."

"What do you mean, 'exactly'? He knows something and they're telling him to keep his mouth shut. And what about the fire on his goddam boat? Same thing. He knew exactly who was setting up Diaz, and they told him, shut up."

"It was Teresa Broadhurst."

"What?"

"She was trying to kill herself. She'd just learned she was pregnant and her boyfriend had dumped her. She went to see Gallagher. Gallagher was gone. She took a bunch of downers and turned on the stove. Then she decided she didn't want to kill herself, and left. She was kind of fuddled. I guess she forgot about the stove. She never told Gallagher."

"How do you know, then?"

"She kept a diary in her studio. I read it this morning. Give it up, Elliot. The man doesn't know."

"You don't know that."

"No. You're right. I'm just guessing."

"And even if he doesn't, he could still find it out."

"No way," Keener said. "No way. You confused me, you know? I thought for a while that was what you really wanted."

"It is."

"Forget it. Once you put your ad in the paper, you blew it. Who'll talk to a guy who's got Feds all over him? And goons. If he starts asking questions, they'll kill him. And they'll kill whoever answers him. No. I thought you were just stupid, Elliot. Now I think you're dangerously stupid."

"And what the hell does that mean?"

"That I know what you're doing."

"Shit," Rossen laughed. "You don't know shit, Keener. And I didn't leak that story, it was you. Maybe you don't even remember you leaked it. Maybe you were drunk. I know all about you. I got friends in Chicago. Insubordination, wasn't that the charge? They could've axed you, but instead they sent you down here where you lushed so hard, they almost axed you for that. So don't mess with me, Keener. You got it? I give 'em the word and you're through. Now as far as I'm concerned, Mr. Gallagher is still under full investigation. And if not by you, then by somebody else. You got it?"

Keener nodded.

24.

At noon, they pulled into Key Largo. For most of the trip Ortega had been silent, sipping at beers, sitting in the sun. His face had turned the colors of a dark rainbow: brown, purple, a weird-looking green. One of his eyes was still swollen half shut. He wore it jauntily, as though it were a wound from an honorable war, but Gallagher still felt the full weight of guilt. Earlier, Ortega had caught him with the guilt, smeared on his face like strawberry jam, and said, "Forget it, amigo. I walked into a door."

"Yeah. Mine," Gallagher had said.

Oretga was sleeping when Gallagher docked. The silence woke him. He yawned, stretched, and then looked at Gallagher, who sat there smoking. "So," Ortega said finally. "What?"

"I been thinkin."

"Yeah. I know. What?"

"Let's go have some lunch."

They walked down the pier. Huddles of sun-bored, sharp-looking kids, barechested, crosses dangling from their necks, glanced at them idly. Grass smoke drifted on the hot, bright air. Gallagher looked at the water. It was green; he thought of Terry's eyes.

The Grenada Cafe was a waterfront dive: gloom and sawdust, tap beer and fish-fry. A couple of ceiling fans whirred overhead. Gallagher ordered from a sea-scarred waiter. "Steamers and a Miller's."

"*Dos,*" Ortega said.

They were silent till the beer came.

Ortega raised his glass. "To fucking the fuckers."

Gallagher said, "To absent friends." He drank. The beer tasted cold and easy. It slid past the giant lump in his throat. "I was thinking," he said, "exactly of that."

"Fucking the fuckers?"

"Yeah."

"Who's the fuckers?"

Gallagher shrugged. "Who isn't? I want to get Elliot Rossen. Rossen's the leaker. First I want to get him offa my back, and then I want to get him. Just get him. You know? And then I want to get Quinn."

"Why?"

"One: he had to know what Rossen's been doing. Two: he didn't give a shit about Terry. He used her and ditched her. He acted like a bastard. Three: he's a hypocrite and hypocrite-bastards shouldn't get to be mayor."

"Right," Ortega said. "So how you gonna do it?"

"I don't know. I keep thinkin what Tommy would have done."

"What would Tommy have done?"

The steamers arrived, swimming in broth. Gallagher looked at them, shrugged. "I don't know. The only time Tommy was in this kind of spot it was different. The mob trusted him. All he had to do was take fifty-seven Fifths."

"Of booze?"

"Amendment." Gallagher laughed. "Couple of times they asked him something tricky and Tommy said, 'I refuse to answer that question on the grounds that I might incinerate myself,' and the D.A. said, 'You mean incriminate,' and Tommy just grinned at him and said, 'Whatever.' "

Ortega laughed. "Sounds sharp, your old man."

"Hell, I don't know. Maybe. Sometimes. Tommy was a gambler, that's all. All his life he was in and out of trouble and money." Gallagher dunked a piece of bread in the broth. "On the other hand, he always got back out of trouble and back into money. I don't know. He had a rule. He said, always go for broke. When you're deep in a hole, you bet everything you got on a longshot."

"Did it work?"

"Mostly. For Tommy. How about you? You got any old Spanish sayings that'd work?"

"Listen, if old Spanish sayings really worked, Mexico would still own half of America. Forget it. Just go with what Tommy would've done."

"Forget it. Tommy would've half-owned Mexico and lost it in a card game."

"But what about Rossen? What would he have done about outsmarting Rossen?"

"I don't know, I don't know." Gallagher shrugged. "Tommy said you never try to outsmart a smart guy. What you do is, you get the guy to outsmart himself."

"Okay. So you gotta bait him then, right? You want another beer?"

"Yeah."

Ortega motioned for the waiter. *"Dos cervezas."*

"I don't know what to bait him with," Gallagher said.

The waiter leaned forward. "Senor? If you want the good advice about bait, you go to the houseboat of Tillie Garcia. Best prices and he give you the fresh live bait."

"We're not goin fishin, though," Gallagher said. "Thanks anyway." He opened a clam and then stared at it. He stared at it hard; then he suddenly laughed. "That's the answer," he said. "My God, that's the answer."

"To what?"

"Getting Rossen. How to get Rossen. It's a longshot, but Jesus, Tommy would've loved it."

"How?" Ortega squinted.

"Like the man just told you," Gallagher grinned. "Live bait, ole buddy. With fresh live bait."

He was making love to her, slowly, on the cool double bed of the boat. And then after it was over he stood, walked away, walked over to the porthole and opened it, stood there lighting a cigarette, indifferent, as though he'd forgotten she was there. She wanted to talk to him, to build some bridge, but she found herself afraid of what she was feeling, of what she might say, and then a doorbell started ringing. He looked at her, smiling, opening a door to what she'd thought was a closet. But a crowd spewed out of it—drunk, very loud, an endless parade of dirty, sneering, sweaty-looking people, and they looked at her and laughed.

The bell kept ringing.

She opened her eyes, feeling a momentary flicker of panic before she realized she was home, in bed, alone, coming out of an incredible dream; and her doorbell was ringing. She looked at the clock: 9:35, and too dark to be morning. She hadn't overslept, just napped. The doorbell continued to ring. She reached for her robe.

"I hear you," she shouted. "Hold it. I'm coming." And

someplace between the bedroom and the foyer, she wondered: was it him?

In the hallway mirror, she caught the reflection of her
drawn-looking face—the slight blue bruise at the center of
her cheek where Gallagher's hand had pressed against her
mouth—and she remembered the dream, the sex in the
dream, and she flushed with the knowledge that that was
what she'd wanted, that the dream had been an accurate
reporter.

At the door, she looked through the peephole.

Alicia stood there, very cool, very crisp. Alicia admitted to being thirty-eight because no one believed it.
Alicia looked thirty; she was probably forty: put-together,
smart. "We're soul-sisters, kid," Alicia once said. Now she
said, "My God, I thought you'd OD'd. Open up. I got
presents."

"Champagne?" Meg looked at the Dom Perignon.
"Christ. I don't think it's a time to celebrate."

"Nope. But it's sure as hell a time to get drunk." Alicia
went into the kitchen for glasses. "Besides, I want to hear
the end of your story. And besides, I'm also bringing you
the news of the day."

Meg sat on the couch. "Did you bring the first edition?"

"In my briefcase." Alicia came back with the glasses
and a towel from the kitchen. Meg opened the briefcase.
"Wait," Alicia said, but Meg was already staring at the
headline.

GALLAGHER INVESTIGATION
STILL ON . . .

She closed her eyes and leaned back. It had all been
for nothing. The whole damn thing had been for nothing
at all.

A cork popped. Alicia nudged her with a glass. "Atta
girl. Open your mouth, close your eyes." Meg opened her
eyes and gulped from the glass. Alicia said, "Slowly."

"Why is the investigation still on?"

"In a word? Rossen."

"What did he say?"

"He said the girl's suicide was—get this—quote, 'regrettable but irrelevant.' He also said that what she told

you was irrelevant. He said she was a mental case. He said she was trying to embarrass her father." Alicia shrugged. "Of course he said it off the record."

Meg held her empty glass out. "What else?"

"What else. Let's see." Alicia filled the glass. "Oh yes. Franklyn Broadhurst is threatening to sue us, but thanks to your pin-mike we've got the lady's True Confessions on tape so we're covered." Alicia settled down on the couch. "Elsewhere in the news, Cavaletti was elected as interim president. What else. Oh yeah. I got to the R and R around seven, and guess who was there?"

"Gallagher?"

"Hell no. Rumor is he left for Tahiti on his boat. Uh-uh. Keener. I don't know if he was looking for you or a hangover. Anyway, he sat there putting them away. Finally he came over to me, very mellowed out, and he told me to ask you, how are things on Tu Do?"

Meg frowned. "What's that?"

"I don't know. I think it's a street in Saigon." She shrugged. "And I still don't know what it means."

Meg shrugged and was silent. She emptied her glass. "You know what he said to me?"

"Keener?"

"Oh, Keener! No. Michael. He said what we do is we strip people naked and throw them to the crowd." She looked at Alicia. "Is that what we're doing?"

"Come on, girl. You're taking Gallagher seriously? Mostly what we do is the other way around. It's the emperor's new clothes that we're stripping. Nixon, for example. Or the sheep's clothing. Lefever, for example. No. What we're showing is the naked truth."

"Yeah. But how do we know what's really the truth? I mean, Jesus, on almost every story you cover, you talk to twenty different people, you get twenty different truths."

"True," Alicia said. "But you do the best you can, that's all." She filled up her glass again and shrugged. "Look. I wouldn't brood on what Gallagher said. He was, to put it mildly, out of control. And besides, if you ask me, it was reeking of Freud."

"Freud?"

"Freud. I think he wanted to take your clothes off because he wanted to take your clothes off."

Meg looked up. "Do you really?" she said.

Alicia was staring at her. "My, my, my. Just look at your expression. Hey, you get off on guys who treat you rough?"

"Of course not," Meg said hotly. "My God. I've never even known one."

"Till now," Alicia said, and lifted her glass.

25.

EYES ONLY MEMO FOR: Keener
             FROM: Golden
                RE: Surveillance of Michael
                     Gallagher, 14 September
                     (Friday)

<u>8 AM</u>   Relieved Agt. Block at the Shoreham Marina, general vicinity of slip 41.

<u>10:47 AM</u> Subject docked boat, Rum Runner II, arriving at marina with John Ortega. Walked to his car. Drove out to 91 Albertson Way where he dropped off Ortega and then drove directly to the National Bank (on S.W. 8th St.), entering the building at 11:08.

<u>11:40 AM</u> Subject emerged, walked 7 blocks west to the Rite Deal Discount Radio Shop, and entered the bldg at 11:44, emerging at

<u>12:08 PM</u> with a sealed brown carton (maybe 2 sq. ft.) He walked to his car, driving to Lauderdale, to 12-97 Poinciana Place—Malderone's mansion, and drove through the gates at 12:43.

<u>1 PM</u>   Subject emerged and drove directly to his house where he stayed, at least until 3:31, when Agt. G. Golden was relieved by Agt. E. Hamilton, who asked me to remind you that he (Agt. Hamilton) has urgent personal appointment at 9 so please don't be late.

INTERNAL REVENUE SERVICE
INTEROFFICE MEMO

FOR: Elliot Rossen
cc: Robert M. Keener
FROM: Edward Bolt
RE: Gallagher, Michael A.
Information subpoenaed from the National Bank

ADDENDA TO MEMO DATED 13 SEPT.

Please note: as of the above date, Gallagher's personal cash assets (all in accounts at the National Bank, Branch 27, on Southwest 8th Street) totaled, as you'll note, $11,286.22.

However, at 11:45 AM, 14 September, bank teller Juan Geraldo Rodriguez (nephew of Carlos Rivera Rodriguez, a minor official of the IDU) voluntarily reported the summary withdrawal of $10,000 from Gallagher's account.

Thought this might interest you.

With warmest personal regards,
Ed

eb: rl

Keener put the file down, picked up his coffee, and looked at his watch. At 4:27 P.M., he noted, his personal coffee consumption for the day was 11,286 cups. Except for the lousy taste of coffee in his mouth, he was feeling okay. His cold was better. He'd awakened with a slight, normal hangover, result of a slight, normal drunk. It had not been a fall-down, punch-out drunk; it had not been an I-don't-remember-it drunk. He remembered it. He'd left the R & R bar (subject emerged at 9:21) and instead of a binge, he'd bought himself a steak and a gallon of orange juice and took himself home. One thing he knew: it was harder to stop drinking than it was not to start. But he'd stopped. He felt pretty good about himself; he'd ridden a tiger. On the other hand, any man who tries to ride a tiger is a suicidal asshole, a fact that his success doesn't alter a bit.

His telephone was ringing. He picked it up. "Keener."
"Yeah," said a husky, whispery voice: Rasmussen.

"Go," Keener said. "What you got?"

"I maybe know where what you're lookin for is."

"Yeah. Well, I'm looking for a few hundred things. Which one is this?"

"Diaz."

"Shoot."

McAdam had the phone between his shoulder and his ear. "How large is the area they're searching?" he said. "Yeah?" He made a note. "Aren't there sharks in that area?" He nodded. "So what's the chance of making an ID if you find him?" He listened. "Uh huh. Okay. Okay. Thanks, lieutenant. I appreciate the call." He turned, ignoring Meg, and bellowed, "Hey, Casey! Ramirez! Get a car and get your ass down to Marathon. Fast. They got a tip and they're lookin for Diaz. In the water." Grinning, he looked up at Meg. "If they find him, we can cut the 'presumed' before 'murder.' " He laughed. "If they don't, what the hell, then the search'll be the story. Christ, you ever seen one? Five thousand spectators gawking at the bay, waiting to see some bloated half-eaten corpse coming up. People," McAdam said, "really stink."

Keener pulled up behind Hamilton's car at 8:47. The street was deserted. He walked up to Hamilton's window. "Anything?"

"Gallagher came out of the house around five, drove to the warehouse, stayed there an hour, came back to the house. That's it. He's been in there since—" Hamilton checked his notebook—"six seventeen."

"Alone?"

"Uh huh."

Keener looked over at Gallagher's house, across the street and two houses down. "Anything else?"

"Yeah. What he bought at that radio store was a whatsitsname, a . . . whaddayacallit, a . . . thing that answers your telephone."

"A telephone answering machine."

"Yeah."

"Technical terms like that are hard to remember." Keener gestured with his chin. "And how about that TV repair truck over there. What do you call that?"

"In technical terms? A green and white panel truck. TV repair." Hamilton grinned at him. "I think it's legit. Guys went in the house there, I don't know, twenty-five minutes ago. What's doing with the search?"

Keener raised his eyebrows.

Hamilton pointed at the car radio. "Twenty guys dragging the water ain't a secret."

Keener shook his head. "They quit it at sundown. They'll try again tomorrow. You better get going if you want to make your date."

Hamilton grinned. "Do I want to make her," he said. "Oh, wow."

Eight fifty-eight. Nothing. Quiet. He opened a deli bag and looked at the sandwich. They'd given him mayonnaise; he'd asked for mustard. Shrugging, he took a bite of the sandwich and looked at the repair truck parked across the street. It was parked out in front of a pink stucco house with a red tile walk and a red tile roof. He looked at the roof.

No antenna.

He put down the sandwich.

Gallagher came out of his house with a letter. The porch light landed on the envelope.

Keener hesitated.

Gallagher started to walk down the block. There was a mailbox at the corner. It was 8:59.

Keener looked quickly at the pink stucco house, number 133, two doors from Gallagher's.

Nothing. All quiet on the stucco front.

Gallagher was walking back from the mailbox, just about approaching 133, as its front door opened.

Keener moved fast.

So did everyone else.

There were two of them. When Keener went zooming past the truck with his .38 drawn and his mouth about to shoot off an "FBI, freeze!" the third piece of muscle came bounding from the truck and tackled him. A really blockbuster move. The bastard was built along the lines of the truck and the gun went flying and Keener went down with the body-by-Fisher on top of him, pounding him. Keener couldn't move. He was saddled and pommeled. He tried to get the angle on to pitch a Sunday punch but the closest he could get was a Wednesday afternoon: nothing. He twisted. Bucking, he rolled; he made it to the top but it didn't last long. A hard knee exploded in Keener's gut and the air went whistling out through his teeth. He fell and the fists were all over him again—a savage backhand left to the face that left him with a kettledrum sound in his head. He tried to get up. The linebacker grinned and raised a ham fist to batter him again, but Keener bolted up and impacted the grin and the muscle went barreling back against the truck where his head hit the door handle.

Down for the count.

The count against Gallagher was two against one—one of them was holding him and one of them was punching and the last thing he saw before he saw a lot of stars was Keener, coming toward him, heading for the puncher.

It was terribly quiet.

He was riding on a carousel without any music.

Painfully, Gallagher opened an eye. Everything was spinning. He closed it again. After a while the carousel stopped. He opened the eye again, opened the other one, and slowly, carefully, lifted his head. He was lying on the grass. Keener was beside him, lying on the grass. Keener looked dead. A trickle of blood was running down his face from a mean-looking puddle on the side of his head. Wincing, Gallagher got himself to move, slowly, rolling over and onto his side. He squinted at Keener. Who still looked dead.

Keener said, "Goddam fucking idiot."

Gallagher grunted and rolled back over. For a while he lay there, staring at stars.

Keener said, "Tell me that didn't happen."

"That didn't happen," Gallagher said.

Keener said, "Good." He opened his eyes. For a while he lay there, staring at stars.

Gallagher said, "I think we better get up."

Keener said, "Yeah."

Neither of them moved.

Keener said, "Does anybody live in that house?"

"Been empty for a month."

"Yeah. . . . You got any cigarettes?"

"No. Left them in the house."

Keener said, "You got any aspirin in the house?"

"Yeah."

"Then I think we better get up."

Keener was sprawled on a leather club chair with his feet on a hassock. Gallagher was stretched out flat on the couch. A coffeepot was sitting on the table between them. Keener's cigarette butt was burning his fingers, but he didn't have the motive or the energy to move. After a while, it became a necessity; he moved, wincing, and then settled back. He looked at Gallagher. They hadn't really messed much with Gallagher's face—just a lot of body blows, stuff that wouldn't show. It showed on Gallagher's face as a grimace.

Keener said, "You happen to know who they were?"

"Nope."

"No shit?"

"No shit. Do you?"

Keener shook his head, a gesture he immediately, profoundly regretted. The timpani section in the middle of his brain started going into riffs. Ka-ka-*boom*, ka-ka-*boom*. He waited for silence. Then he said, "Out-of-town talent, I guess."

"Yeah. Maybe."

"So what did they say?"

"Nothing."

"Come on. That kind of music has words with it."

"Yeah." Gallagher hesitated, shrugged. "Okay. They said, 'The next time you talk, you get dead.' No. Let me do that again. They said, 'The *next* time you talk, you get dead.' Like I'd already talked."

"Uh huh." Keener thought about that one for a second. He nodded.

Gallagher was watching him. "Shit. Is that telling you something?"

"Yep."

"Want to share it?"

"Nope."

"You're a bastard."

"Yep. Want to step outside and repeat that?"

Gallagher laughed; then he moaned. "If you make me laugh again, I'll kill you."

Keener leaned forward and poured some more coffee. It was wonderful coffee. "What you told me," he said, "is that a tip we got earlier is probably good. And they think you're the tipper."

Gallagher looked at him. "Tip about the body?"

Keener just shrugged.

"Christ. How the hell would I know about the body? I don't know anything."

"Yeah? If I were you, I'd try to sell that to Santos."

"How? Put my hand on the Bible and swear? You know what that'd get me?"

"Yeah. Broken hand."

Gallagher was silent.

"What are you planning with the ten thousand bucks?"

Gallagher turned, looking blank and perplexed.

Keener shook his head. "Skip the dummy act, pal. It's a federal law. Every bank in the country makes a standard report to the IRS on any transaction of ten grand or more. You know that."

"They report it in the first half an hour?"

"What the hell," Keener shrugged. "Point is, we'd know about it sooner or later. What's going on?"

"Maybe I'm buying a ticket to Rio."

"Maybe you're buying a contract. Maybe you're buying somebody off."

"I don't think so. Do you?"

Keener shrugged. "You're something. You're up to something, aren't you."

"Nope. I got a tip on a horse at Hialeah."

"Hialeah isn't open."

"Yeah. That's exactly why it's such a good tip. Only horse on the track."

Keener laughed, sipped his coffee. "Christ, this is good. How the hell do you make it?"

"You start with this blend of Jamoca and—"

"Forget it. Never mind." He lit another cigarette. "I ought to get moving." Keener didn't move. He finished his coffee and put down the cup. He stood, slowly. "I'll get you off the hook with your uncle," he said. "At least about yesterday. At least I can try."

"How?"

Keener shrugged.

"Why?"

Keener shrugged. "That's a goddam good cup of coffee," he said.

26.

FEDS DRAG BAY FOR DIAZ'S BODY

MARATHON, Sept. 14. The search for the body of Joseph Diaz in the cold green waters of Florida Bay north of this fishing village on the keys has yielded nothing in its first few hours. According to Lt. Harold Camillo of the Marathon police, the search began late on Friday afternoon when a local diver, whose name has been withheld, saw what he described as part of a body

Keener read the Saturday paper at noon. He picked up the telephone and dialed Camillo.

"Thanks," he said.

"*Nada*. But you owe me one, Keener."

"Hell. You owe *me*. If we find that body, it's you gets the credit."

"Yeah." Camillo laughed. "Yeah. Guess you're right."

Keener hung up. The phone rang instantly, under his hand.

Hamilton barked at him, "Christ, I don't believe this. I'm at a phonebooth in a fucking mosquito-ridden campsite in the Everglades."

"Why?"

"Because Gallagher's here. I tailed him."

"Okay. So what do you want from me? Mosquito repellent? Hazard pay? What?"

"Don't mess with me, Keener. I'm being eaten alive. I got news that's gonna blow your ear off."

"Try."

"He's meeting with Quinn."

Keener watched his ear fly straight out the window. *"What?"*

"You heard me. I'm afraid to get close, but he's across the canal on one of those islands at a picnic table and he's talking to Quinn."

"Harrison Quinn? You sure?"

"Six-two, about two hundred pounds, light brown hair, smilin brown eyes, age thirty-seven—"

"Harrison Quinn."

"That's what I thought. So what do you make of it?"

"Son of a bitch."

"Who?"

"Take your pick."

"Your move," Quinn said. "You called the meeting."

Gallagher nodded. "Yeah. I want to deal."

"What are you dealing?"

"Whatever I can get." He squinted as Quinn sat taking that in greedily. The handsome ham-actor face looked pleased. He wondered what Terry had seen in it.

"Deal how?"

"No federal witness stuff. I stay in Miami. I never testify. I only deal with you."

"And what do you expect in exchange?"

"I want the investigation of me over. Now. And I want a statement in the press clearing me."

"Oh. I see." Quinn chewed his lip. "What do you think you can find out?"

"Whatever it is, it'll be more than you got—which is nothing."

Quinn nodded thoughtfully. "Yeah. But we don't make statements clearing people, Gallagher. It's never been done. We don't talk about any investigation till someone's been indicted."

"But someone sure talked about this one, didn't they."

"It wasn't my office."

"Who knows you're here?"

Quinn said, "No one. You said you wanted this private." He slapped a mosquito that was buzzing at his ear. "Why come to me?"

Gallagher laughed. "Why? I'm being hurt, that's why. I'm in a bind. And I wouldn't trust Rossen as far as I could throw the Astrodome."

"So. I'm the lesser of evils, is that what it is?"

"What did you expect? A love letter? Look, I'm trusting you, Quinn. And you know what'll happen to my neck if this leaks."

"It won't." Quinn batted at another mosquito.

"Make sure of that. Don't tell Rossen you met me."

"Why? You think it was Rossen who leaked? You're wrong. It was Keener."

"Then don't tell either of them."

Quinn raised his shoulders. "Mike, I can promise you absolutely that we'll finish the investigation right now. I'm just not sure about the statement to the press. It's too . . . unusual."

Gallagher stood. "Then there's nothing to talk about." He held out a piece of bright yellow paper. "Here's a number you can leave a message at. When I read what I want in the papers, get in touch."

Quinn looked at the number. "I'll see," he said slowly. "I'll have to give the matter very serious thought."

On Sunday the *Times-Gazette* was delivered as well as a copy of the *Chronicle-News,* and the best way to read through all of that paper was to spread it on the floor. She was lying on the floor surrounded by paper. Reading the *Times-Gazette* was instructive, Meg always found. It was interesting to see how the two different papers would cover the same exact information, though often the information was different. In a recent robbery, just for example, the *Chronicle-News* reported three million dollars worth of jewels had been stolen by four masked men. The *Times-Gazette* had it at four million dollars and three masked men and, according to which of the papers you read, the vault was on the third or the second floor, and the watchman had been brutally beaten unconscious or was merely asleep.

Joseph Diaz remained in the news, even though there wasn't any news about Diaz. Both papers gave it the same headline. SEARCH FOR DIAZ BODY CONTINUES. The town of Marathon was fifty or forty-six miles from Key West, and the rescuers had sweltered in ninety or ninety-six degree heat, but either way, they hadn't found any body.

The doorbell rang.

She hated it when people came by without calling, and she almost didn't answer. She walked to the door and quietly opened the peephole.

"Gallagher?"

He shrugged in the hallway. "Messenger," he said. "I'm making a delivery." He held up a package.

She opened the door. He was beautifully dressed in a beige linen suit. She looked at her own misbegotten outfit: blue cotton shorts with coffee stains on them and a stretched-out T-shirt. And unwashed hair. She looked back at Gallagher. "What are you delivering, another sermon, or an arsenic pie?"

"Why don't you let me in and find out?" His blue eyes gave her a smooth, level look.

She nodded. "Sure. Want some coffee or something?"

"No." He followed her in, looked around. "Are you training a puppy?"

"Am I what?" She followed his glance to the floor, to the carpet of papers. "Oh," she said. "No. Busman's holiday."

"Oh."

She shrugged. "You want to sit down?"

"No. Thanks." He paused. "I was pretty rough on you Thursday and I—"

"Don't," she said quickly.

"Don't what?"

"Apologize."

He shook his head. "Wasn't going to. I just wanted to, uh, set the record straight a little. I think you ought to know this. It wasn't the first time Terry tried to—I mean, she'd tried to kill herself a few times before."

"Thing with the airplane?"

"Yeah. You do do your homework, don't you. Yeah. And once before that, and then I think about a month ago she tried it on my boat. I'm not sure about that, but I—well, it kind of figured. It was after—"

"Michael?"

"What?"

"Don't tell me. Don't tell me any more. I'm a reporter, Michael. Don't forget that. Please."

"Oh, Christ. Don't you ever stop being a reporter?"

"How can I?" She looked at him. "Same pair of eyes, same pair of ears. I can't just turn them off at six o'clock Friday. So I just don't want you to—"

"And how about your mouth? You ever turn *that* off?"

She laughed. "I don't seem to be able to, do I." He was standing very close to her, watching her mouth. "Got any suggestions?"

"Yeah. Chew gum." He held up the package. "I owe you this," he said.

"What is it?"

"A blouse."

"Oh." She looked at the package: Saks. "I'll get you your sweater."

"Sweater?" He frowned. "Oh. Nicky's."

She opened the closet.

"Hope it fits," he said.

"It's gotta fit better than the sweater did."

"Huh?"

She handed him the sweater.

"Oh," he said. "Yeah. I see what you mean."

"Saw," she said quickly. And flushed.

He nodded. "Your mouth's bigger, though." He moved forward again, stood close to her again. They were silent for a moment.

"What I told you," she said. "About Rossen. Did it help?"

"Yeah. Maybe." He shrugged. "We'll see."

"Yeah."

He nodded, started for the door. "So, uh, maybe I'll see you one of these days."

"I'd like that."

"Would you?"

"Yeah. Would you?"

He looked at her. "I think . . . Jesus, it'd sure be complicated, wouldn't it?"

"They're the best kind."

He said nothing, kept looking.

She flushed again. "Your decision," she said. "Your move."

He nodded. "I'll give it some serious thought."

27.

Keener was looking at a rack of magazines at the lobby newsstand when O'Leary came in, followed by a guy with a television camera. Right behind O'Leary was another anchorman, another mini-cam, another guy with lights, and Keener got the message that something was up.

Keener stopped looking at the rack of magazines, and started to look at the straggling, two o'clock, back-from-lunch crowd. He spotted Delgardo (The *Times-Gazette*) Kenworthy (ABC Radio News), and watched them walk toward the back of the lobby and then disappear through a door at the rear.

Keener was only mildly curious. Crews would descend on the Federal Building like The Charge Of The Camera And Light Brigade, but Keener knew the major story of the day depended not so much on the story as the day. If trains didn't crash, if banks weren't robbed, if nobody famous got married or shot, then some poor slob who'd embezzled a few hundred bucks from his boss would get himself promoted to page one news. Keener went back to considering *Playboy* and whether it was really worth two bucks a shot. He spotted Meg Carter moving toward the counter. She was wearing her hair swept up in a puff and she had a kind of high-necked Victorian blouse. She looked like a girl on a cameo: sweet, old-fashioned, and perfectly poised. She bought a pack of cigarettes and started away.

"Lookin good," Keener said.

She turned, surprised, then stared at him. "And you look absolutely awful. My God. What happened?"

"Oh." He ran a hand on his lacerated cheek, shrugging. "I fell."

"Off the wagon?" she said.

He squinted. "What makes you think I was on it?" He started to walk with her, crossing the lobby.

"It didn't occur to me at all," she said, "till I heard

you were off it. I heard you were looped in the old R and R. And then I remembered. All those Cokes."

He nodded. "When in doubt, attack, is that it? What's pissing you, Meg?"

"I heard you were calling me Saigon Sue."

"Where'd you hear that?"

"Bartender. He's been repeating it a lot. He seemed to think it was funny."

"And you don't."

"No."

He suddenly smiled. "She scars at jests."

"You weren't jesting."

"Nope. I was mad. I went to question a girl in the morning and I found her in the bathtub."

"And you think it's my fault."

"I don't think it's that simple."

She stopped. They were standing by the gilded Justice. "You want to call a truce?"

"Why? It's just a fencing match, it isn't a war. Just good clean sport." He smiled at her again. "You'll be late for your conference."

"Quinn," she said flatly. "I bet it's political. He wants to assure the people of Miami that even though he's running like a demon for mayor he isn't neglecting his duties."

"Is that what the handout says?"

She shook her head. "No. My personal bet."

He looked at his watch. "Okay. I'll walk you out to the casino," he said.

There were forty reporters waiting in the courtyard, sweating in the sun, and clustering around a flag-draped platform. Keener stayed behind, leaning on a wall, while Meg moved forward, pushing through the crowd.

Quinn arrived promptly at 2:17, only two minutes late. He looked dapper and trim. He walked to the platform holding a single piece of paper in his hand, a prepared statement. He read from it quickly.

"I have a short——very short—statement to make. The Organized Crime and Racketeering Strike Force has recently completed an investigation of Michael Anthony Gallagher with regard to his possible involvement in the disappearance of Joseph A. Diaz and has found no grounds to proceed any further against Mr. Gallagher. Because this investigation was inadvertantly reported in the press, it is the feeling of this office that it's only proper to acknowledge its conclusion." He looked up from the paper. "That's it. I have no further comment to make."

Meg started grinning. She ran through the doors to the lobby phonebooth. Dialing, she looked at the wall plaque of Justice. "You saw it," she said.

The phone rang twice.

"This is Michael Gallagher."

"Michael?" she said, but his voice kept talking.

"I'm not here at the moment, but, uh, if you want to leave a message, you can wait till you hear the beep and then talk."

She found herself frowning. For a man who'd made a point about absolutely hating to talk to a machine, it was odd that he'd bought one.

She hung up the phone.

Shiloh and Bolt were already seated on Rossen's sofa when Keener ambled in.

"You're late," Rossen said. He was pacing the room. For a moment he was silent, then he said suddenly, "You see this rug?" He pointed. "Quinn just pulled it out from under us. And what I want to know is, I want to know why." Rossen looked at Keener. Keener said nothing. Rossen looked at Bolt. "You got any ideas?" Bolt looked at Keener. "No?" Rossen suddenly paced to his desk and picked up a memo. "Fine. Then you're both idiots," he said. He was flashing the memo in front of their faces. "See? See? It says right here: from Edward Bolt, carbon to Keener."

Keener lit a cigarette.

"Gallagher withdrew ten thousand dollars on Friday afternoon. On Monday afternoon, Quinn pulls the rug out."

Bolt dropped his jaw. "You think Gallagher *bought* him?"

"I don't know," Rossen said. "I don't know, but I smell it. There's fish in the air. Quinn knew exactly what we were doing. He gave me his tacit approval, okay? Something changed his mind. Something changed his mind between Thursday and Monday, because Thursday he told me he was with me all the way."

"Did he?" Shiloh said.

"Tacitly. Tacitly," Rossen said. "Yes. He agreed with me the Broadhurst abortion meant nothing. That it wasn't worth pursuing. That she might have made it up. So something's cooking. Something's cooking and it stinks like cabbage."

"I thought it was fish," Keener said softly.

Rossen glared at him. "Cabbage meaning money. I want it checked out." He looked over at Bolt. "I want to find out, what did Gallagher do with that ten thousand bucks?"

Bolt shrugged. "He might have hidden it under the mattress."

"Fine. Then I want his mattress looked under. And I want Quinn's mattress looked under."

Shiloh said, "You don't have cause for a search warrant."

"So? So? I got cause for surveillance. Right? And the rest of it, you figure out. Look, don't you see it? We get both of them. Conspiracy. Obstruction of justice. And then we got Gallagher right where we want him. He'll play or he'll tumble for a hard-time twenty. Or both," Rossen said. He looked up at Keener. "Surveillance and a phone tap. A tap on both of them. Gallagher and Quinn."

Keener said, "You'll never get permission for a tap. It's a—"

"Right. And we're not gonna ask permission either. That's red-tape bullshit." He turned back to Shiloh. "Surveillance and a tap."

Shiloh was silent.

"So spend a few dollars, will you?" Rossen said. "It's the taxpayers' money, not yours, for Christ sake. And I'm telling you, we're gonna make some history here."

"All right," Shiloh nodded.

"Twenty-four-hour."

"All *right*," Shiloh said. He looked sideways at Keener, who looked at the wall.

Keener handed Hamilton a couple of cigars. "Rossen,"

Keener said, "just gave birth to a bird. I think it was a screaming eagle."

Hamilton shrugged. "But Rossen could be right."

"Christ, I'd hate to think so," Keener said slowly. "I'd sincerely hate that." He lit a cigar.

Hamilton was thinking. "Gallagher gave Quinn a piece of paper," he said.

"Huh?"

"At the picnic table. When they met."

"Was it green? Like a crisp ten-thousand-dollar bill?"

"Cute. Very funny. It could've been a check. A cashier's check?"

"Was it? Did you see it?"

"No. I was hiding in the bushes with binoculars. You see the mosquito bites on Quinn this afternoon?"

"Yeah." Keener swiveled in his chair again, thinking. "And Rossen doesn't even know about the meeting. Neither does Shiloh." He drew on his cigar. "I'd like to keep it that way."

"Are *you* obstructing justice?"

"Officially? No. Officially we weren't tailing Gallagher, remember? Shiloh told us not to."

"I don't know. I don't like it," Hamilton said.

"And I don't like phony phone taps, either."

"What's your angle?"

"Obtuse."

"Come on."

"I trust Gallagher a lot more than Rossen. I honestly believe the guy doesn't know beans and that he couldn't find it out, and it's just possible he convinced Quinn of that, too."

"Ten thousand bucks is a powerful persuader."

Keener looked up. "Quinn isn't that dumb. I don't *think* he's that dumb." Keener thought again. "Maybe he is. Maybe Gallagher is. Maybe I am. Maybe the whole country is. Maybe all our brains have been rapidly destroyed by vermillion food dyes and television waves. You ever think of that?"

"You're changing the subject."

"Fuckin A. I don't want Rossen to be right, that's all. You know what's the oldest surviving species, the oldest surviving species in the world? The roach. Elliot Rossen is a roach. The human roaches are winning, taking over. I don't like it. I hate it. You can't walk down the street without a fuckin can of D-Con. Look, you want to know about Elliot Rossen? Rossen doesn't want justice, Rossen wants credit. He came to Miami in seventy-seven. I'd been here for a year. It was a bad year, but forget about that. Rossen comes in all shiny and new and he wants to make a case, a big one. Okay. Fair enough. So he goes after Gallagher—Tommy. Okay. Still fair enough, but he goes after him stupid. He's giving out immunity like it's measles vaccinations. Everybody line up and stick your arm out. He's dealing with every piece of scuz in every jail in Florida and he gets it, he builds up a pretty tight case, and what happens then? Tommy Gallagher dies. He's screwing a redhead and his heart conks out, and there goes Elliot's best-laid plans. His career stopped there. His reputation as Bright Boy ended on the spot. And that's why he wants to get Gallagher now."

Hamilton was quiet. He lit the cigar and then looked up at Keener. "But he still could be right."

"I know," Keener said. "But I want to make sure before I give him any glory."

Gallagher awakened to a young Doris Day making black and white eyes at a young Rock Hudson and realized he'd slept through the six o'clock news.

He punched the button on his answering machine and listened to a total of eleven hangups, a wrong number, a message from Nicky saying it was six and she was leaving the office and going to her mother's and adding that she hated his goddam machine, and a message from Ortega:

"Yeah, uh, shit. Are you there . . . ? Oh . . . okay. Listen, I'm going to the dog track, amigo. Want to come? Uh, call before seven if you do. Uh . . . there's a long-shot in the second race. Twenty-eight to one. How's that for a longshot? The only trouble is, I think it's a dog."

The doorbell rang.

Gallagher froze. He wasn't sure if he should answer it at all, or whether he should answer with a smile or a knife.

It was possible Santos hadn't really believed him on

Friday afternoon. It was also possible that Santos had believed him but Cavaletti hadn't. Anything was possible.

He peered through the window.

A teenage kid was standing on the porch. "Mr. Gallagher?"

"Yeah?"

He was holding an envelope. "For you."

"Letter bomb?" Gallagher said.

"Huh?" The kid frowned. "It's from the *Chronicle-News.*"

Gallagher nodded. "Letter bomb," he said.

He opened it slowly.

A note was stapled to what looked like a copy of a newspaper page.

> Michael—
>
> This is tomorrow's page one—just in case you cancelled your subscription. I'm happy for you.
>
> Meg

He lifted the note and unfolded the page:

GALLAGHER NOT INVOLVED

IN DIAZ CASE: QUINN

And the byline:

By Megan Carter

He read the article, then looked at his watch: twenty after eight.

She was sitting at a booth with Alicia when she saw him moving past the bar, coming toward her. He hesitated, lighting a cigarette, and Meg said, "Alicia, your nose needs some powder."

"Huh?"

"Take a powder."

"Huh?" Alicia turned, saw Gallagher. "Oh." She nodded. "Oh. I think I'll go to the powder room," she said. And went.

He stood there, leaning on the wall.

"You just happened to be in the neighborhood," she said.

He shook his head slowly. "I'm not really sure this is a good idea."

"Some of the best ideas aren't good."

He nodded.

She stood.

8:23, Hamilton wrote, *Gallagher drove to the R & R Bar. 8:47, went into the bar. 8:51, came out of the bar with Megan Carter, drove to his house, followed by her. 9:11, entered. Together.*

He handed the notebook to Keener. "That's it."

"Uh huh." Keener read it and looked at the house. No lights. He nodded.

"Maybe they're watching television, huh?"

"Shut up," Keener said.

"Does it bother you?"

"Just shut up," Keener said. It bothered him. Not very much. But it did. But not very much. He glanced at the street. No mean-looking cars. No trucks. "No goons?" he said to Hamilton. "Not that you'd know one if you saw one."

Hamilton ignored him. "He hasn't had a tail since Friday afternoon."

"Except us."

"Except us." Hamilton nodded, getting out of his car. Yawning, he stretched. "Kind of makes you think, doesn't it."

"What?"

"Think he told Santos he was buying off Quinn."

Keener just grunted.

"Kind of makes you think he's got money hidden someplace, doesn't it? Shit! He owes every penny in his business account. He wouldn't leave himself with only twelve hundred bucks. He's gotta have a cash box someplace, doesn't he?"

"You'd think so," Keener said.

"You wouldn't?"

"Yeah. I would. I'd think so." Keener looked at the street. "Only, if he had a cash box, that's where he'd have taken the money from. Christ. Why from the bank where it's traceable? Why?"

"Because he's not very smart?" Hamilton offered.

"That, or very."

"So what does that mean?"

"I haven't," Keener said, "the vaguest fucking idea." He looked at his watch. "Got a date tonight?"

"Yeah." Hamilton laughed. "Stew. Irish stew. Aer Lingus. Hey, look, she's got a friend with her. German. Blond. Not bad. If you want me to—"

"I'll think about it," Keener said.

"Hell. What's there to think about?" Hamilton shrugged, getting into his car.

She woke in darkness and blinked, not remembering where she was. And then she rolled over and he came into focus, lying beside her, his eyes wide open, smoking a cigarette.

"Supposed to be the other way around," he said huskily.

"Mmm?" She ran her fingers down the center of his chest—nice, broad, hairy chest.

"Supposed to be the guy falls asleep right after."

"Time is it?"

"Quarter of midnight."

"Oh." Her finger circled a bad-looking bruise. "Catnap."

He cupped her chin in his hand. "Curious cat."

She grinned at him. "I'm very happy," she said. "I am quite incredibly impossibly happy."

"I know," he said.

"You know?"

"Mmm-hmmm."

Keener was hot and thirsty. He pulled out a stick of gum. There was only so much liquid you could drink when you were doing a stakeout. Try relieving yourself in the gutter or the bushes and it turns out to be the exact same moment some little old lady comes walking her dog. So you kept an empty bottle on the floor of the car. And then if you used it, the car really stank. So Keener popped some Trident gum in his mouth. The night was muggy.

Crickets chirped in the dark bushes. Gallagher's house was quiet and dark.

A silver Dart turned into the street. It pulled over, parking in the space in front of Keener. A woman got out.

He recognized her instantly.

"Nicole," he said softly as she walked by his car.

She stopped, turned, looked at him uncertainly.

"Don't," he said.

She cocked her head at him. "Don't what?"

He shrugged.

She stood there, perplexed, in the moonlight. She frowned. "What the hell are you doing here?" she said. "The news just said the investigation's over."

He nodded.

"Then what . . . ?" She walked over to the car and leaned through the window. She brought with her a faint aroma of spice. She was dressed in green—pants and a shirt—and her red hair was braided with a green velvet ribbon. She looked like Christmas. "Is he still in danger? He told me what happened here Friday when those muscles tried—" Her eyes ran over Keener's crudded-up cheek; they suddenly softened. "Does that hurt?"

He shook his head. "Looks worse than it feels. No. There's no particular danger."

"Then why . . . ?" She turned, looking over at Gallagher's house. At the second car in the driveway. "Oh."

For a moment she was silent, staring at the car. The moment stretched; she couldn't seem to move.

"Want a cigarette?"

"No."

"Want a drink?"

"Yes." She turned to him. "What've you got?"

He held up a thermos. "Orange juice?" he said.

She laughed. "What the hell," she said, and opened the door.

She licked her fingers, leaning back on the pillows. "You make a mean chicken, Gallagher. You want that leg or can I have it?"

"I don't want *that* leg," he said.

She laughed. She was probably, he thought, the only girl in the world who could laugh with her lips smeared

with lipstick and chicken grease and still look beautiful.
He poured some more wine. She sipped it. "This is good."

He put the bottle on the bed tray. "Lafite. Sixty-one."

She pointed at her mouth. "La mouth. Fifty-four. I
guess I'm always putting Lafite in la mouth."

He shook his head slowly. "Boy, you are fast."

"Too fast for you, Gallagher?"

"Nope." He picked the bottle up, filled his own glass.
"Collector's item."

"Really?"

He nodded, watching her, wondering what in the hell
he was doing.

"Celebrating," he said.

She lifted her glass. "To Harrison Quinn. Who proves
there is justice in the Justice Department."

"Jesus." He laughed.

She looked at him, surprised. "That was really a damn
decent thing he did today."

"Christ." He laughed again.

"What's so funny?" she said.

"Nothing. Everything." He drank, laughed again. "Me.
You."

"I don't get it," she said.

He nodded. "I know."

Nicky filled a plastic cup with the juice. "Sure you
don't want some?"

Keener shook his head. Her hair brushed against him
as she moved. "You okay?"

She nodded. "No."

Keener lit a cigarette.

After a while she said, "Thank you."

"For what?"

"Not saying something stupid."

"Oh."

She was silent again for a moment, looking at the
house.

Keener said, "It probably doesn't mean a thing."

"Shit. You just said it."

"Something stupid?"

She nodded.

"You in love with him?"

"No. Maybe. I don't know. But I'm sure as hell feeling like hell." She shrugged. "I'm really not as tough as I look."

"I never thought you were tough."

"Didn't you?"

"No."

"Oh."

He smiled. "Sorry."

"Most people think so."

"Most people don't think at all." He turned; his eyes checked the street. "How's your brother these days?"

She looked at him sharply. "My God! Did you even go and question my brother?"

He shrugged. "Had to. Had to find out about the Colt thirty-eight."

"How did you—"

"Your mother. We were checking what happened on the day of the fire. She said you and Gallagher went down to see your brother. That you were worried about him. That he's in a wheelchair and some guys had roughed him up and his store had been robbed. A few days later your friend buys a gun and a few days after that, you go back to see your brother."

"And from that, you—"

"It was a hell of a longshot," Keener said. "I just thought there was a chance he might've bought it for your brother."

"He did."

"I know. I'm not as stupid as I look."

"I never thought you were stupid."

"Just boring."

She laughed. "What's your first name?" she said.

"Bob."

28.

Transcript of a telephone conversation between unidentified male and Michael Gallagher's answering machine (on his home telephone), Tuesday, 18 September, 9:40 AM.

MACHINE: This is Michael Gallagher. I'm not here at the moment, but, uh, if you want to leave a message, you can wait till you hear the beep and then talk.
MAN: This is, uh . . . you know who this is. We should talk. Get in touch.

Note: In the opinion of Agent G. Golden, the unidentified male above is Harrison Quinn. Suggest conducting a voice-print test.

The following is a transcript of a telephone conversation between Michael Gallagher and Megan Carter. Call placed to Gallagher's warehouse phone, Tuesday, 18 September, 10:50 AM.

CARTER: Hi. You were sleeping when I left.
GALLAGHER: Yeah. I guess. What time did you leave?
CARTER: 8:30.
GALLAGHER: Oh. Well, wait until you're my age. You can't stay up till 4 and get up at 8:30.
CARTER: You can sure stay up. I'll say that for you, kid.
GALLAGHER: Jesus, there you go again. The mouth.
CARTER: I meant it as a compliment.
GALLAGHER: Yeah. It was a nice night, Megan. I enjoyed it.
CARTER: So did I. I kind of forced that out of you, didn't I.
GALLAGHER: No.
CARTER: Why I called was, I think I left my earrings on—

GALLAGHER: You did. Do you need them in a hurry?
CARTER: No.
GALLAGHER: We'll get together, then. Later in the week. Okay?
CARTER: I'm free every night except Saturday.
GALLAGHER: How about Saturday?
CARTER: (laughs) Okay.
GALLAGHER: See you.
CARTER: Bye.

CONFIDENTIAL MEMO TO: Edward Bolt, IRS
                       Robert Keener
             FROM: Edward Hamilton
          SUBJECT: Gallagher, Michael A.
ENCLOSURE: Photograph, cashier's check.

A reliable informant provided me the enclosed photo and the following info:

Michael Gallagher has, at present, in a locked metal box in a desk on his boat, a cashier's check from the National Bank, made out in the sum of $5000 payable to The Committee for a Better Miami and signed by Roger M. Claus of the bank. The date on the check is 14 September. The serial # is 792-212841.

"Reliable informant, like hell," Keener said. "You went on his boat."

Hamilton shrugged. "And pulled out a plum."

"And stuck your thumb in your ass. You get caught doing that and—"

"I didn't."

"Uh huh. How'd you get on the boat, break and enter?"

"Just enter. The hatch wasn't locked."

"It wasn't?"

"Nope."

"I see." Keener nodded.

"I don't think you're seeing a goddam thing. I don't think you're seeing the goddam check. Will you look at that check? Do you know what that means?"

"I know what it looks like. I just don't like the way you got it, that's all."

"Well, Shiloh doesn't mind. He told me to do it."

"Terrific. You're going over my head."

"Aw, shit," Hamilton said. "No. Shiloh went under it. He came to me directly."

"Yeah. Okay. I get it. All right. The rest is up to Bolt." Keener swiveled in his chair.

Hamilton stood there. "Are you mad at me?"

"No. But you're mad at me."

"Yeah. I am, now that you mention it. I want to know who the hell's side are you on."

Keener swiveled again. "You think it's that simple? You really think it's Blackhats and Whitehats?"

"Yeah! Basically, yeah."

"Well I'll tell you something, Eddie. You get enough dirt on your hat, it turns black."

INTERNAL REVENUE SERVICE
INTEROFFICE MEMO

FOR: Elliot Rossen
         cc: Victor Shiloh, Robert M. Keener
FROM: Edward Bolt
    RE: Gallagher, Michael A.
         Information subpoenaed from National Bank, 21 September.
ENCLOSURE: Photostat, cashier's check, serial # 792-212841.

National Bank vice president Roger M. Claus remembers signing not one, but *two* $5000 bank checks for Michael A. Gallagher on 14 September, *both* made out to The Committee for a Better Miami.

Further, on 19 September, the first check cleared, cashed by the Manufacturer's Bank (Branch 21; 3280 Biscayne Blvd.), the bank of record for the CBM.

Thought you'd want to know this.

                              Best,
                                    Ed.

*   *   *

The following is an edited transcript of a conversation between Agent R. Keener and Addison Karp, treasurer of the Committee for a Better Miami. Karp is 67, retired partner in Commager and Karp, Public Accountants. Interview conducted 21 September (Friday), Karp's office at Committee HQ.

KEENER: I believe sometime this week, possibly on Monday, your office received a bank check for $5000. A contribution.

KARP: No.

KEENER: You say that without hesitation.

KARP: (laughs) Sir, I assure you, if we'd gotten any check for $5000, I'd know about it. No. In the first place, for tax purposes, most checks don't exceed—

KEENER; Yeah. Well the problem is, you did get the check. It's already been cleared.

KARP: I'd say that's impossible. What's the purpose of your line of questioning, sir?

KEENER: Routine investigation of a possible donor. I can come back with a warrant but, uh, well, I know your committee stands for law and order and I thought—

KARP: Whatever I can do for you, sir. But there wasn't any check.

KEENER: Would you call your bank and confirm that?

KARP: Certainly, sir. First thing Monday.

The following is a transcript of a telephone conversation between an unidentified male and Michael Gallagher's answering machine, Saturday, 22 September, 9:20 AM.

MACHINE: (Standard speech)

MAN: (very husky, gravelly voice) Our boy's gettin nervous. I think he wants a meet. I think you better stop at the bakery first.

The following is a transcript of a telephone conversation between Michael Gallagher and Megan Carter placed from the telephone on Gallagher's boat, Saturday, 22 September, 10:40 AM.

CARTER: Hello?

GALLAGHER: Yeah. We had a date on tonight.

CARTER: Yeah. Do we still?

GALLAGHER: Sure. But I thought we'd start early, okay? Take the boat down to Bimini.

CARTER: How far is that?

GALLAGHER: Three or four hours. Thought we'd leave at noon.

CARTER: And come back at night?

GALLAGHER: Yeah.

CARTER: Is that safe? I mean, uh, to be in a boat in the dark?

GALLAGHER: Jesus. Tommy used to do it all the time. You scared?

CARTER: I'll meet you at the pier around noon.

Keener read the notes and looked up from the page.

"That's it," Golden said. "Do we tail him to Bimini?"

"Yeah." Keener nodded.

"And who's 'our boy'? The one that wants the bread? Quinn?"

"I guess we'll find out," Keener said. "You want to do the tailing?"

"No. I want to take my kid to the beach."

"Hamilton'll go. He'll take his little stew on the seaplane."

"Yeah." Golden sighed. "Christ. To be single."

Keener just looked at him. "Go," he said. "Take your kid to the beach."

He was waiting on the boat. As she walked down the pier, she thought about the other times she'd been on the boat. The first crazy time. The second crazy time. Maybe she was crazy. She'd been nervous all week, expecting him to call, just to say hello, but he hadn't, and she'd found herself looking at the phone as though it were a plastic instrument of torture. She wondered if she'd told him too much the other night, confessing that she'd felt so incredibly happy, or whatever she'd said. Or maybe he'd known she'd left her earrings on purpose. Stop it, she told herself. Stop it right now.

He smiled at her, lifted her onto the boat, and then, to her surprise, he didn't hold her, didn't kiss her; he just said, "Hope you brought a bathing suit with you."

She nodded, disappointed.

"Go change," he said briskly. "I got a little work to do before we take off."

She went down to the cabin, remembering the last time she'd been in the cabin, and her dream about the cabin. And, again, *Guys and Dolls* was playing on a tape. She started undressing, looking at herself in the mirror in the head; she looked like a woman who didn't know what in the hell she was doing and was doing it anyway. No. Wrong, she told herself. Wrong. It was sex, that's all. It couldn't be more. More would be stupid. Dangerously stupid. She pulled on the top of a flowered bikini and the tape started playing "I'll Know When My Love Comes Along."

To hell with it. She did not want to fall in love with Michael Gallagher. Therefore, she wouldn't. Easy as that.

The engines started, drowning out the music. She climbed to the deck.

The following is a transcript of a telephone conversation between Nicole Peralta and Michael Gallagher's answering machine, Saturday, 22 September, 1:50 PM.

MACHINE: (Standard speech)
PERALTA: Oh Christ. The machine again. Umm, it's Nicky. Yeah, uh . . . Listen. Remember that Japanese stereo thing? The one you told me to buy and you told me you'd put it together when it came? Well, it came. I want to read you the first instruction: "Please to require the careful fixation of red wire A onto slot RQ, not touching, but firmly, blue wire C." I think I need help, Michael. Call if you're around.

"That's it," Cole said. "I'm knockin off for the beach. Want to come?"

Keener looked at his watch. Two-thirty. He shook his head no.

"Come on," Cole said. "You look like you haven't seen air in a year."

Keener stood up. "Got something else to do."

                    *   *   *

"Meg, this is Charlie Wilson. Charlie, Meg."

She looked up at Gallagher.

The old man was hollering over the engines. "I think we met before."

Gallagher looked at her with innocent eyes. "Charlie's comin' with us."

She nodded. "Hi, Charlie," she said. "How's it goin?"

Keener stood on the front porch for two entire minutes before he rang the bell.

She answered the door in shorts and a tube top. Barefoot, she was tiny, five-one, he decided, and he felt not only like a jerk, but a big one.

She cocked her head at him.

He shrugged. "I was just, uh . . . The thing is, I had another question to ask you."

She turned and looked over her shoulder.

"If you've got company," he said quickly, "I can come back later."

"No. I was thinking the house is a mess. I'm trying to put this stereo together and I—" She shrugged, moved back. "Come on in."

He looked at the "mess" on the floor: components, screwdrivers, cartons, an ashtray loaded with butts. "Having trouble?" he said.

She laughed, rolled her eyes. "Want a pineapple milkshake? I got some in the blender."

He nodded, and watched her moving to the kitchen. He settled on the floor and picked up the booklet: *Please to require the careful fixation* . . .

He found wire A and slot RQ. He was putting them together when she entered with a tray.

"You're *doing* that?" she said.

He nodded, took a milkshake and put it on the floor; he kept on working, silently.

"So what was your question?"

He looked at her. "Got a pair of scissors?" he said.

Following is a transcript of a telephone conversation between an unidentified male and Michael Gallagher's answering machine, Sunday, 23 September, 11:40 AM.

MACHINE: (Standard speech)
MAN: Tahiti Beach. Thursday morning. 11 AM.

EYES ONLY MEMO FOR: Rossen, Shiloh, Keener
            FROM: Golden
              RE: Surveillance of Michael
                     Gallagher, 23 September
                     (Sunday)

<u>8 AM</u>   Relieved Agt. Block at the corner near Gallagher's house.

<u>10:20 AM</u> Subject emerged. Drove to Gittler's Bakery (947 Collins Avenue). Entered bldg. 10:41, emerged 10:50 with bakery bag. Drove to the home of John Ortega, entering bldg, 11:08.

<u>1:20 PM</u>   Subject emerged, drove back home, entering the bldg at 1:58.

<u>2:17</u>   Subject emerged, walked to the mailbox immediately adjacent to surveillant's car. Mailed an envelope, walked back home, entered the bldg at 2:19. No further action.

CONFIDENTIAL MEMO FOR: Edward Bolt
               FROM: Robert M. Keener
          SUBJECT: Cashier's check, serial
                     # 792-212841
           CASE #: 75-27

Addison Karp, Treasurer, Committee For a Better Miami, says the check had been mailed directly to his bank and was cashed automatically. Please check further.

INTERNAL REVENUE SERVICE
INTEROFFICE MEMO

  FOR: Robert Keener
FROM: Edward Bolt
  RE: Your memo 24 September

Manufacturer's Bank (Branch 21) confirms the statement of Addison Karp. Details will follow. Best—

Ed

cc: Elliot Rossen

"Have we got him?" Rossen said, "or have we got him." He was shooting off rubber bands again, not even aiming, just shooting. "That was Quinn. That was Quinn. His voice on the tape. 'Tahiti Beach. Thursday, eleven.' So that's when they're meeting. And Gallagher put another check in the mail. We got 'em." He laughed, turning to Shiloh. "Did I tell you this would pay, or did I tell you this would pay?"

Keener said, "The messages are only on tape. You can't prove that he got them."

"Bullshit. He got them. And the proof'll be we catch him at the beach on Thursday. Right? I want pictures. Lots of them. Send your boy whatsisname. Hamilton. He does a good job."

29.

It wasn't a beach day. It was cloudy. The radio was promising rain, and the first few drops of it were starting to fall. Gallagher right-turned onto the road that headed to PARKING: TAHITI BEACH. The lot was deserted. He looked at his watch. 11:02. A garbage truck was sweeping the edge of the lot. A bad-looking bruiser got out of the truck and emptied a pail full of beer cans and chewed-over hot dogs and rolls. A hot dog vendor was calling it a day, hitching his wagon to the back of a Beetle. That was it. And the rain was really hammering now. Eleven-oh-eight. He started to wonder if he'd made a mistake, if he'd been too smart. He wondered if Quinn had to cancel the meeting and had phoned. In that case, the caper was blown. The number he'd given to Quinn had been Charlie's—the yellow wall phone on Charlie's boat—and he'd told Quinn to call it from a telephone booth. The messages he'd left on his own machine—his own imitation of Harrison Quinn and the possible apex of his acting career—had all been a blind. If the phone had been bugged, and he was damn sure it was, a voice scan would prove that it hadn't been Quinn. But if Quinn had called Charlie this morning to cancel while Gallagher was already driving to the beach—

Quinn's car was pulling into the lot.

It moved next to Gallagher's, nose to tail. Quinn was rolling down a window, quickly.

Gallagher grinned at him. "Hi."

Quinn nodded. "You got something for me."

Gallagher shrugged. "Yeah. It was a pretty professional job."

Quinn just glared at him.

Gallagher stuck his hand through the window and caught a few raindrops. "There's talk it might've been some guys from Nevada. Out-of-town talent, you know what I mean?"

"I know," Quinn said. "The Cavaletti theory. That was even in the papers, for Chrissakes. Listen—"

"So maybe the papers were right."

Quinn leaned forward. "Go on," he said eagerly. "What did you learn?"

"Nothing."

Quinn just stared for a moment, then he turned purple. "What the hell do you mean? I got my neck stuck out for you from here to Haiti and you're givin me '*nothin'*? What the hell do you mean?"

Gallagher shrugged. "Hey. You guys been on the case for two months. I been on it a week."

Quinn raised his hands to heaven. "My God! For this you call me out to the beach in the rain? Listen you, I need something. Hear me?"

"I hear, I hear."

"So make sure you hear something soon. You hear?"

"As soon as I hear, you'll hear from me."

"Jesus!" Quinn said. "For this you call me out to the beach in the rain. *Jesus!*" he said, and rolled up the window and started the car.

Hamilton said, "How's that for a shot?" He tossed down a picture: Quinn with his neck stuck out in the rain. "I think I'll become a photographer. Lookie." He tossed down another photograph. "Man, it was even worth hiding in a garbage truck for. But Jesus Christ, did I stink last night."

Keener just nodded. He looked through the file. Sur of the file. The file was now about six inches thick.

"And the second cashier's check cleared at the bank. Gallagher's check. Five thousand bucks. Paid to the committee that's bankrolling Quinn."

Keener just nodded. He looked through the file Surveillance reports. The photos of the checks. The phone calls: "This is . . . you know who this is. We should talk . . ." "Tahiti Beach. Thursday. Eleven." Pictures of Gallagher and Megan on the boat. Megan half-naked as he ripped off her skirt. Pictures at Bimini. Megan and Gallagher. Megan, Gallagher, and Charlie Wilson . . .

"Rossen wants to call a grand jury next week."

Keener looked up.

"Rossen says we got him. Come on, Keener. Say something. And don't give me that shit about roaches. Nobody's perfect. We nailed a badguy. We nailed two. And we couldn't've done it if we'd played by the rules, and you know it."

Keener said nothing. He was looking at the file.

"You know what's wrong with you?" Hamilton said. "You're a fuckin Boy Scout."

Keener said nothing. He was reading a report.

RE: Surveillance Michael Gallagher
    28 September (Friday)

His eyes skimmed down the page to the final entries, an hour ago:

11:28 AM   Subject emerged from cabin of boat in bath-
            ing suit. Stayed there, reading on the deck,
            and was there, reading, at 12:42 when Agt.
            Golden relieved by Agt. Block.

"Hello?"

"Is this Charlie Wilson?"

"Yep. Who's this?"

"Bob Keener. Remember me?"

"Federal fella."

"Yeah. Let me talk to Gallagher, will you?"

"Ain't here. On his boat. Got a phone number there. I'll give it you."

"No. I want to talk to him here. On *your* phone. Tell him."

"Okay," Wilson said.

Keener waited. He poured himself a stiff double Cutty and took it to the couch. He wasn't used to his apartment on a Friday afternoon. It seemed to look different in the weekday light. He looked at the scotch in the weekday light, in the weak-day light, he thought, put it down, picked it up again, looked at it.

Gallagher's voice said, "What's going on?"

"That's what I want to know and I want to know it fast. Otherwise your trick blows up in your face."

"What trick?"

"I got the checks, I got the phonecalls. I also got the pictures of the meeting, okay? You got exactly what you wanted."

Gallagher said nothing.

"And none of it'll stand up in court," Keener said.

"So?"

"So nothing. So nothing at all. Quinn gets off and then Rossen gets off. You paid ten thousand bucks and you bought yourself nothing."

Gallagher was silent.

"Hey, you understand? Nothing. Rossen takes it to a grand jury. Jury throws it out. But grand jury testimony has to stay secret. Nobody leaks it or it's automatic jail. So Rossen makes an ass of himself for a couple of hours in front of a grand jury and that's it. End of story."

"Oh."

"That's all you got to say to me: 'oh'?"

"Oh, shit."

Keener was silent. "Your move," he said finally.

"Move where? To Alaska? I got twelve hundred bucks." Gallagher laughed. "Well, what the hell. I was playing a longshot and it didn't come in."

"Race isn't over."

"How?"

"We're only rounding the clubhouse turn. Talk to me, Gallagher."

"Tell me something, Keener."

"What?"

"Why the hell are you telling me this? What makes you think things aren't what they seem?"

"Character. A question of character. Most people are pretty consistent. They do the same kind of action again and again."

"So what the hell is it I'm doing again?"

"Punching the Justice Department in the jaw."

Gallagher laughed. "Well, I'll be goddamed. You're right."

"Fuckin A. Your move," Keener said. "Talk to me, Gallagher."

"And then what?"

"Then?" Keener said. "Then it's my move." Shrugging, he poured the scotch on the floor.

*   *   *

It was dumb. In the last few months she'd begun to feel edgy whenever she parked in the underground garage. It was stupid. And it wasn't stupid at all. The woman in Apartment 6A had been robbed here; so had the couple in 17J and old Mr. Paulsen in 22R and the girl whose apartment was right across from Meg's. The management, which charged an exorbitant rent, had decided not to hire a security guard but instead had installed electronic devices that either seemed to jam or to not work at all.

Meg pulled her groceries out of the car, slammed the door with a whack, locked it (a car had been stolen here, too), and was starting to move across the dark quiet floor when a shadow started moving from the shadow of a post and she stopped, held her breath. It was the shadow of a man, a very tall man, or a very tall shadow; it was ominous. She told herself to keep on moving, and she tried to move quickly in another direction—a direction that would lead her away from that post.

Her heels made an echoing click on the floor.

But the shadow moved too.

She started to run.

A voice said, "Meg?"

She sighed her relief, turning.

It was Keener, looking rumpled and loose. His jacket was off, his shirtsleeves were rolled, and he didn't have a tie. He leaned against the post now and lit a cigarette, right beneath the sign that said Smoking Forbidden $50 Fine. He said, "Sorry if I scared you."

"What the *hell*," she snapped, "did you think you'd be doing? Sneaking up in the—"

"I thought you'd like the Deep Throat setting." He clicked off his lighter. "I mean, didn't they meet in an underground garage? I mean Burnwood and Wordstein?"

"Are you drunk?"

Keener laughed. "Honey, you don't even know what drunk is." He laughed again. "Uh-uh. Sober as a judge." He shrugged. "Sober as a judge who's had two double Cuttys. That's all. I want to talk to you. Deep Throat style."

She frowned. "About what?"

"About Rossen. He's busy lowering the net, and you're gonna get caught in it."

"What net? Come on. The investigation's over."

"And the party's just beginning. Rossen's about to nail Gallagher and Quinn. I want you to nail Rossen. This is not for attribution. If you quote me, I'm finished."

She shook her head quickly. "I don't follow. I don't know what you're—"

"I'm talking about dirty tricks, you understand? In the Justice Department. Starting with a bogus investigation and ending with illegal wiretaps and a lot of—"

"Wait a second. Roll that back. Gallagher and Quinn. What about them?"

Keener hesitated. "There's a certain amount of evidence indicating Gallagher"—he looked at her—"you can't quote me on this."

"All right," she said quickly.

"No. Repeat: 'I will not put your name on this, Keener. I will simply call you a knowledgeable source.'"

"I will not put your name on this, Keener. I will simply call you a knowledgeable source."

"Then c'mere a minute."

"Where?" she said suspiciously.

"Aw, Jesus. You think I'm gonna rape you? I'm not that fast. Your boyfriend's coming over in twenty-five minutes."

"How did you—"

"I just told you. His phones have been tapped." Keener opened the door of his car. "There's a file there," he said. "Look it over. Keep in mind what I've been telling you. Illegal phone taps. Illegal search. I'm gonna walk around the block. When I'm back here, you're gone, but you leave me that file. If you have any questions, I think you know the number."

She nodded, got into the car, started reading.

There was something in the air. Onions frying, for one thing. But as Gallagher entered the apartment and looked at her—the way she was biting her lip, the way she didn't meet his eye—he knew something was cooking, and not just in the kitchen.

"Smells good," he said slowly. "What is it?"

"Stew."

"Oh. You sure it's not a kettle of fish?"

Her eyes scanned him quickly.

"I just wanted to be sure I brought the right kind of wine."

"Oh." She'd started to move towards the kitchen. "What did you bring?"

"Chateau Pichon LaLande. The first of the new crop. It's supposed to be good. You want to try it now?"

She shrugged. "Sure."

"Then I have to have a corkscrew." He followed her into the kitchen.

She opened a drawer. "In there," she said, and turned the beef in the skillet. She went back to the counter and started chopping carrots.

He opened the wine. He wondered what had happened. When he'd called her this morning, she'd been openly pleased. He'd asked her to dinner and she'd said, "Hey, look, I got a better idea." He'd been calling from the warehouse. Ortega walked in and heard what he was doing and looked at him blackly. When he hung up the phone, Ortega said slowly, "You are lobed out, amigo. You are totally nuts. Do you know what you're doing?"

"What am I doing?"

"I don't know. Do you?"

And Gallagher had thought about it, shrugged. "She's beautiful."

"Yeah. Both faces. What else?"

He shrugged again. "So maybe she's another longshot I'm playing. Maybe I'm betting that, uh . . . I don't know. There's something warm in her. I've seen it."

"Sucker bet."

"Maybe. We'll see."

He looked at her again. She was silent and tense. The only sound in the kitchen was the chopping of carrots and the frying of meat.

"Tastes good," he said.

"Huh?"

"The wine." He filled a glass, held it out to her.

"Oh." She glanced at it. "No. Thanks."

He nodded. "Then spill it, okay? Tell me what's on your mind."

She turned to him, the nub of a carrot in her hand. "All right," she said. "Quinn. When he cleared you, did you know he was going to do that?"

He looked at her levelly. "No." Which was true.

"He didn't tell you?"

"Uh uh." He sipped at the wine. "I thought I'd take the boat out to Nassau this weekend. Want to come?"

"With Charlie?"

"Nope. You and me."

She turned again, started chopping carrots again. "Why do you think he had a press conference, Michael?"

"Huh?"

"Quinn. Why do you—"

"What're you, workin?"

"They don't usually do that, you know. Announce the end of—"

"Oh, yeah. I remember. You don't turn it off at six o'clock Friday." He looked at his watch. "Too bad. Six-thirty."

She moved from the counter, facing him. "I'd like to know the truth." She waited. He shrugged at her. "Please," she said urgently. "Tell me the truth."

"You? Or the paper?"

"What difference does it make. The truth is the truth—isn't it?"

"Uh uh." He shook his head. "No. There's all kinds of truth. Those six blind men describing the elephant. *They* told the truth. Remember? One of them touches the trunk and he says, 'Hey! An elephant's just like a snake,' and another grabs the tusk and he says, 'It's like a spear.' Christ. That's the kind of truth *you're* telling, Megan. Not the truth, but what other people *tell* you is the truth. And me? I'm not gonna tell you, okay? So you better decide for yourself who I am . . . and who you are." He watched her.

She said nothing for a moment, then lifted her shoulders. "Just tell me something. Just tell me one thing. Quinn's statement. Did you do—did you do something wrong to get it?"

"What's 'wrong'?"

"You know goddam well what's wrong."

"Yeah. But do you?" He looked at the bottle. "You still

need to check out the label, don't you. Someone labels me bad, you're gonna go by the label."

"Just tell me—"

"No. I'm not talkin to the *Chronicle-News.* 'No comment,' is what I tell the *Chronicle-News.*"

"Tell *me.*"

He shook his head. He put the glass on the counter. She was watching him. He ran his hand lightly through her hair. "Things aren't always what they seem to be, Megan. Not always. Don't you know that?"

She lowered her eyes. "But they usually are."

"Okay," he said briskly. "Okay."

She watched him as he walked through the hall. She heard the door close behind him, and she stood there for a moment, staring at the wine bottle, looking at the label. *Récolte 1981.*

She picked up the phone, dialed, waited.

"Mac? It's me. I've got a story . . ."

30.

Cardigan said, "In my humble, but extremely expensive opinion, it's dangerous."

Edwards was chewing his thumb. He didn't look rested from his two-week vacation. Edwards worked terribly hard at everything, even at relaxing. "Which part of it?" he said.

"I'm not, as it happens, concerned about Quinn. The man, beyond question, is a public figure. I've had a rather lengthy discussion with Miss Carter and, again, I'd say we're provably absent of malice. The strange investigation of Harrison Quinn is printable." Cardigan looked up at Meg. "However, what concerns me is the rest of the story. The accusations of an unnamed source. These are serious allegations of grave misconduct in several branches of the Justice Department, and—"

Edwards cut him off. "All right." He turned to Meg, nodding. "I've been doing some checking on your source. I'm sorry, but I'd say he's unreliable, Meg. The official word on him is, insubordinate. Problems with authority and problems with liquor."

"Oh." She considered that. "Yeah. Well, I'd say he was a little bit drunk. I don't think he'd have come to me otherwise."

"So." Edwards nodded. "But the file?"

"It was real. The checks, the phonecalls, the pictures of the meeting."

"Yes. Exactly." Cardigan nodded. "And to cover ourselves, I'd suggest we handle it exactly as we did on the other, remarkably similar occasion. All we report is the ostensible fact of an investigation of Harrison Quinn, attributable only to a 'knowledgeable source.' You did, Miss Carter, get a comment from Quinn?"

She nodded. "Yeah. I called him at home. I think I woke him up. He denied that he'd ever accepted any bribes or had any illegal dealings with Gallagher. He said he couldn't believe he was the subject of investigation. I assured him he was, and he said, 'My God, there's been a terrible mistake.' "

Cardigan nodded. "And Gallagher?"

"Gallagher refused to comment."

"I see. Have you talked to anybody else?"

"Yes. The Committee for a Better Miami. I had Ammico call them."

"And what did they say?"

"It was Broadhurst who said it. At first he denied any knowledge of the checks, and then he said—wait." She looked at her notes. "Here: 'However, if that should be the case, the Committee would immediately withdraw its endorsement of Harrison Quinn.' " She looked up at Edwards.

He laughed. "We've got enough of a story right there." He turned to McAdam. "Let's go with it, Mac."

Quinn was awakened on Sunday morning when a two-pound newspaper fell on his chest.

Melanie said, "Good morning."

He blinked, looked down at the paper. The headline screamed at him.

HARRISON QUINN: SUBJECT OF
PROBE ON BRIBERY CHARGE

Quinn closed his eyes, but he still felt Melanie's glare on his face.

"Ten thousand lousy dollars?" she said.

"You wouldn't believe me if I said it wasn't true?"

She laughed. "It doesn't matter much, does it? You're finished."

"Not quite," he said. "No." Turning, he dumped the paper on the floor. "But if I am, my love, I'll still have one consolation."

"What?"

He looked at her; grinned. "So are you."

Nicky said, "My God. What's she doing to you now? And why the hell are you laughing?"

He kept on laughing. "Keener," he said.

"Keener? He told her this?"

Gallagher nodded, still laughing. "He must have."

She frowned. "Oh, Jesus. I thought he was . . ."

"What?"

"Never mind."

Gallagher studied her. "No," he said slowly. "Keener's just fine, just fine."

She looked at him.

"Believe me," he said, and started laughing again.

Keener read the paper at a drugstore counter. It seemed he'd been reading everybody right. He wondered if Megan had believed he was drunk. She probably had; he'd played it, and the lady believed what she saw—or whatever she wanted to see of what she saw—and he'd figured her correctly. Character. People did the same things again. Over and over. Gallagher had touched her and therefore she'd had to push Gallagher away. Over and over. Again and again. As Keener was repeating Chicago again. Only this time he'd been in a no-lose position. If she'd printed the story he'd given her—the real one, the one about Rossen and his rotten M.O.—it would have gone faster, but not any better.

He chain-lit a cigarette and stubbed out the butt. This way was better. Slower, but only by a couple of days. And quieter. And Keener wouldn't have to leave town.

He looked at the counterman. "Play it again."

"Huh?"

"Another cup of coffee," he said.

31.

The following is a transcript of an informal investigative session conducted in Conference Room 221 of the Federal Building, Miami, Florida, 3 October.

WELLS: Well now. Let the record show that I am James J. Wells, assistant attorney general for the organized crime division of the United States Department of Justice. With me is, uh, United States Marshal Elving Patrick. Also sitting right here at this table is, uh, quite an impressive bunch. We've got, uh, Victor Shiloh and Robert M. Keener of the FBI, United States Attorney Elliot Rossen, United States District Attorney Harrison Quinn. And then we got with us a Ms. Megan Carter, a reporter for the *Chronicle-News* and her attorney Mr. —sorry, what's your name, counselor?
CARDIGAN: Cardigan, Josiah Cardigan.
WELLS: With a t or a d?
CARDIGAN: D. Cardigan.
WELLS: Oh yeah. Like the sweater. You all buttoned up, Mr. Cardigan? (laughs) Also with me is a Michael Gallagher, who says he's in the liquor business. I have had no conversation with any of these people prior to the beginning of this record. At this time I am informing all present that each of them has the right to remain silent and a right to retain counsel. I inform them further that anything they say in the course of this, this, what the hell is this? this inquiry may be taken down and used against them. So much for Miranda. I never liked any of her movies anyway. All that dancing and the fruit in her hat. Anybody here want a lawyer?
ROSSEN & QUINN: (both shake their heads no)
WELLS: I'd like that for the record. Mr. Rossen?
ROSSEN: No.
WELLS: Mr. Quinn?
QUINN: No.

WELLS: Ms. Carter, you brought your own. Mr. Gallagher?

GALLAGHER: No.

WELLS: We got no more room here, anyway. All right now. This paper I've got in my hand. The Chronicle-News. I guess everybody's read it. They got a story here says the strike force is investigating a U.S. district attorney, suspecting bribes. Damndest story you ever did read. So what we're gonna do is, we're just gonna sit here and talk about things. Of course if you get tired of talking up here, Mr. Elving Patrick will hand you one of those subpoenaes he's got and we'll go down and talk to a grand jury. Talk all day if you want to, but you better talk truth because I promise you something: come sundown there's gonna be two things true that aren't true now. One is the U.S. Department of Justice will know what the hell's going on around here, and the other is I'll have someone's ass in my briefcase. Is that understood? Let the record please show that nobody answered to the contrary here, but on the other hand nobody answered at all. All right, Elving. Give whichever one of these guys you want a subpoena, and we'll go downstairs.

QUINN: Mr. Gallagher's a government witness.

WELLS: Wonderful thing, the power of subpoena.

QUINN: He's working on Diaz. He's reporting to me.

ROSSEN: (to Quinn) Your arrangements include campaign contributions?

QUINN: What the hell are you talking about?

ROSSEN: I'm talking about ten thousand dollars. Cashier's checks. (to Wells) You'll find the two photostats there in the file.

QUINN: What file?

WELLS: Mr. Rossen's investigation file. Let the record please show that I'm holding up the file.

QUINN: Let me see that.

WELLS: I'll save you the looking, Mr. Quinn. Says you met with Gallagher, didn't report it. Says Gallagher gave money to some committee that thinks you're pretty. Got some phone taps, none of them legal, mind you, of you talking to Gallagher's answer machine.

QUINN: (to Rossen) You sonofabitch!

WELLS: Well, well. He don't think much of your investigation, Elliot. Doesn't like illegal phone taps, I guess. (to Quinn) How come you didn't report any meeting?

QUINN: That was Gallagher. Those were his rules. He said he'd only deal directly with me. We'd had a leak—

WELLS: Leak? You call what's going on here a leak? Last time there was a leak like this, Noah built himself a boat!

QUINN: Look, I don't know anything about any cashier's checks. Gallagher said he'd listen for us if we'd quit hassling him. He wanted a public statement—

ROSSEN: And you sure as hell gave it to him!

QUINN: Yeah, that's right, Elliot. Gave. I didn't sell it. And I didn't do what you did, which was try to get him killed. You were using him as decoy. Admit it.

WELLS: Mr. Rossen?

ROSSEN: That's a crazy paranoid charge.

WELLS: Is that your answer?

ROSSEN: Yes.

WELLS: Let the record show the question wasn't answered. (to Shiloh) Who gave you the authority to run those taps?

SHILOH: I, uh, no one.

WELLS: Disappointed in you, Victor. You got a pretty good record. Why'd you do a nincompoop thing like that?

SHILOH: It was just, well, it seemed—there was reason to believe—

ROSSEN: He was acting on my instructions.

WELLS: He don't get paid to act on your instructions. He gets paid to enforce and abide by the law. Elliot? How come you're investigating a D.A. without telling the department?

ROSSEN: Well, it was just preliminary. We had cause but no case.

WELLS: You think you got a case now?

ROSSEN: I think so.

WELLS: Fine. Then go ahead. Make it.

ROSSEN: Here? Now? In front of them? (indicating Carter and Cardigan)

WELLS: Hell, you know something that isn't in the

papers already? Go ahead. Pretend you got a grand jury here.

ROSSEN: (to Wells) You want to hand me the file?

WELLS: Let the record show I handed Mr. Rossen the file.

ROSSEN: Mr. Gallagher, you know Mr. Quinn pretty well?

GALLAGHER: Not well, but I know him.

ROSSEN: And how do you know him?

GALLAGHER: He wants me to find out who killed Diaz.

ROSSEN: Mr. Gallagher, I'm showing you photostats of two cashier's checks drawn on the Florida National Bank and made payable to the Committee for a Better Miami. Have you seen them before?

GALLAGHER: Yeah. They're mine.

ROSSEN: Yes. For what purpose did you make these checks.

GALLAGHER: To help the committee.

ROSSEN: Yes. And why would you want to do that?

GALLAGHER: They do good work.

ROSSEN: Are you aware that the committee is backing Mr. Quinn for mayor?

GALLAGHER: Yeah.

ROSSEN: And?

GALLAGHER: It's okay with me.

ROSSEN: Let me point out that the checks are both dated September fourteenth, and that one check was mailed immediately before your first meeting with Mr. Quinn, a meeting which resulted in a public statement clearing you of any involvement with Diaz, and the second one was cashed immediately after your second meeting.

GALLAGHER: So?

ROSSEN: So what do you make of that?

GALLAGHER: Nothing.

ROSSEN: Nothing? Was the committee aware of your donations, Mr. Gallagher?

GALLAGHER: They got the money, if that's what you mean.

ROSSEN: They got the money because you sent it directly to their bank. But they didn't know who sent it to them, did they?

GALLAGHER: I hope not.

ROSSEN: Why?

GALLAGHER: Because a lot of people think I'm a criminal. It was even in the paper that I might be a killer. It'd make them look bad, taking a criminal's money. So I made it anonymous.

ROSSEN: Yeah. Bullshit. You were paying off Quinn.

GALLAGHER: You prove it.

ROSSEN. If, Mr. Gallagher, you did in fact make a deal with Mr. Quinn that you'd act as an informant, then what information have you given him?

GALLAGHER: None. Things are tight. People don't want to talk.

ROSSEN: And what about the messages from Quinn on your tape? And what about the message (reading from file): "Our boy's getting nervous. I think he wants a meet. I think you better stop at the bakery first." What does that mean?

GALLAGHER: That wasn't from Quinn.

ROSSEN: About him.

GALLAGHER: No. This friend of mine, he likes the bagels from Gittler's.

KEENER: I can back him on that one. It's also in the record. The following morning he stopped off at Gittler's and went to see a friend.

ROSSEN: But the messages from Quinn—

GALLAGHER: Never got them. I don't know. It's a lousy machine. I got it at this crummy—

QUINN: You sonofabitch! You're trying to frame me. He set me up. He arranged the meeting. He phonied the machine. He made the checks out. He's trying to frame me.

ROSSEN: Why? What's his motive?

QUINN: He's getting even. You, you and your phony investigations! You pulled one on him, so he must have figured you'd pull one on me.

WELLS: Mr. Gallagher? Hell, are you really that smart? I see. Uh huh. Let the record show Gallagher didn't respond but looked at Mr. Keener, who looked at the ceiling. Something nice on the ceiling, Mr. Keener?

KEENER: A crack.

WELLS: Ms. Carter? You seem to know a lot about

what's going on. I'd like to know the source of these interesting stories.

CARDIGAN: Objection. My client is under no—

WELLS: Save the objections, counselor. We're not in a courtroom. Now, Ms. Carter. The story about Mr. Gallagher, the first one?

CARTER: I had reason to believe the strike force was investigating him. I confirmed it and I wrote the story.

WELLS: And how did you confirm it?

CARDIGAN: Objection. That's asking my client—

CARTER: Just a minute. I'm going to answer that question. I read the file.

WELLS: Did you now? A file from the Justice Department. And how'd you do that?

CARTER: Well, I had an appointment with Elliot Rossen. When I got to his office, Mr. Rossen wasn't there. But, uh, the file was. It was right on his desk.

WELLS: Did you ask him what the hell he was doing, leaving his files around for you to read?

CARTER: No. But I think he intended me to read it.

WELLS: Why?

CARTER: Because he wanted me to write that story. To compromise Gallagher. I didn't know the government worked like that.

WELLS: The government doesn't, Ms. Carter. And this second story here. He gave you that, too?

CARTER: No.

WELLS: Who did, Ms. Carter?

CARTER: I'm sorry, Mr. Wells, but I can't tell you that.

WELLS: Ms. Carter, I think I know where we're heading. Before we get there, let me tell you something. You know and I know that we can't tell you what to print and what not to. We hope that you people in the press will act responsibly and when you don't, there ain't a hell of a lot anybody can do about it. But we can't have people wandering around leaking stuff for their own reasons. It's not legal. And worse than that, it's not right. Now I can't stop you, but I can damn well stop them. I want to know where that story came from.

CARDIGAN: Under the First Amendment, my client is not required to reveal her source of information.

WELLS: Horse pucky. That amendment don't say that,

counselor, and the privilege don't exist. Ms. Carter? You understand I can ask you in front of a grand jury?

CARTER: Yes.

WELLS: And if you don't answer there, you can go on to jail?

CARTER: I know it's possible, yes.

WELLS: It's more than possible, Ms. Carter. It's likely. Now I'm not anxious to be locking up reporters, but I don't like what's going on around here.

CARTER: Can I say something? I don't want to go to jail, but this has to stop someplace. A lot of damage has been done. And a lot of it's my fault. I know that. I wrote a story that was true. It just wasn't true enough. Then I wrote a story that was—that was too true, I guess, more than someone could live with. I keep thinking, there ought to be rules. I mean, rules about what I ought to do. But there aren't. I, I guess I just have to decide. I—the person who told me that story, I think the person's motives were—to straighten things out, to have a meeting like this. I think the person wanted, well, in a way, what Mr. Gallagher wanted, justice. Actual, simple justice. I, I don't want to go to jail. I'm terrified of jail, but if I tell you who it was you'll have to do something about it. And somebody else will be hurt. So, maybe it's simple. I can hurt someone, or I can not hurt someone. No rules. Just me. I'm sorry, Mr. Wells. I can't tell you.

WELLS: I see. Mr. Keener, you got any comments?

KEENER: About what?

WELLS: The weather. The price of gasoline.

KEENER: Oh. The lady's taking a very noble stand. I think she ought to think about it carefully.

CARTER: I have.

WELLS: Mr. Gallagher? Hell. I sort of want to ask you if you set all this up, but if I do, I don't exactly reckon you'll tell me, would you? Yeah. I didn't reckon. All right. You're excused now, sir. Oh. Just wait before you open that door. You come up with anything on this Diaz business, you give us a call.

GALLAGHER: I'll do that. Good-bye.

WELLS: So long. Ms. Carter? It was nice meeting you too.

CARTER: Does that, what about the grand jury and—

WELLS: I don't think so. No. I've got a little work for you to do today, anyway. Something you should write. You're not gonna like it very much. It'll say Mr. Quinn, while he isn't the smartest D.A. in the world, is not so dumb as he's suspected of being. It'll say there isn't any evidence he's suspected of anything. It'll say that you yourself personally got suckered by Mr. Rossen here, who has some pretty peculiar ideas about how to do his job. And it'll say it was premature and just flat-out wrong that these stories ever got reported in the press. Now you don't have to print it, of course. But I still plan to say it, all of it, at a press conference here in just about an hour, and they tell me when I make a statement, it's news. So go have yourself some lunch and be back in an hour. I think that concludes this, whatever it was.

"Hey, I heard you did good," McAdam said.

She shrugged. "Maybe. I . . . I don't know," she said vaguely. "But I think I did . . . right."

"There's a difference?"

She nodded. "Yeah. I think so." She sat in her desk chair and picked up a pencil. "So what happens now?"

"Now?" McAdam grunted. "We pass out the tap shoes. I think we got a lot of fast dancing to do."

She shook her head slowly. "I'm so sorry, Mac."

"Yeah. Well. What the hell. How it goes."

"It hardly ever goes quite as badly as this."

"Yeah. True."

She studied her thumbnail. "How do you want me to handle it?"

"I don't."

She looked up.

"I want Alicia to handle it. Hey, look, I gotta tell you this. You're not gonna love it, but Cardigan says we gotta cover it."

"What?"

McAdam lit a cigarette. "Gallagher and you. Cardigan says he saw pictures in that file that someone could blast us with. I mean, to the moon. The only protection is if we do it first."

"I don't under— Why?"

McAdam laughed brusquely. "In the second place, it's

news. In the first place, Quinn could try to use it against us. Gallagher framed him and you wrote the story. Conspiracy. Malice."

Meg shook her head at him. "But Michael didn't—"

"Tell you? Sure. But go prove it. I mean if you were a jury and you looked at those pictures—"

"Oh."

"Yeah. Oh. Cardigan said if we word it very carefully, we don't have to worry. Much. He said Quinn very likely won't sue us. But the third-place reason is our own credibility. As of this moment it's totally shot. So the thing is, we gotta have a sacrificial lamb."

"I see."

"Sorry."

She shrugged. "How it goes."

"Yeah."

"So I really made the paper look bad."

"You made the *press* look bad. And Meg, I better warn you. Every paper in the country'll get onto this wagon. They'll have to. They'll have to defend their own honor. Proclaim their own policies. Assure their own public. You're gonna be some red-hot news for a while. If I were you, I'd go spend a month in Alaska."

"You mean I'm not fired?"

"Maybe. I don't know. We'll have to see how it goes."

"Oh."

"Hey, look." McAdam sat on her desk. "This'll all blow over. All of it. Believe me. Everyone survives. Rossen'll survive. Quinn'll survive. All the guys from Watergate got rich writing books. Whatshername—the one who lost the Pulitzer Prize. I read she's getting courted by the publishing houses. They said if she can write such prize-winning fiction she ought to write a novel. Everyone survives. The press'll survive. It's survived a lot worse. Hey listen, when I started out in this business everybody knew that reporters were bums, and once in a while the surprise was we weren't. And you want to know who the hell ruined it for us? Edward R. Murrow. Woodward and Bernstein. Bastards like that. Christ, they made reporters look fatally upright, like ducks in a goddam penny arcade. And then everybody takes a shot at us. Blang! Win a stuffed teddy bear. Things turn around. They always turn

around, Meg. Shit. The country used to believe in poli-
ticians. Remember? And we used to trust scientists too.
And businessmen. And then we trusted nothing at all.
And then for a minute there, we trusted the press. And if
right now the press is in the mud heap, remember,
things'll turn around. They always turn around, and when
the rest of those bastards do something really rotten, we'll
find it, we'll expose it, and we're back on the top. So have
a cup of coffee, go clean out your desk, and by the time
you're getting back from Alaska, who knows? Maybe
we'll find another Pentagon Paper."

"Jesus," Meg said. "That's a hell of a speech."

"Yeah. I think I'll run for mayor," Mac said.

32.

It was sunny, but the air was breezy and dry. She walked along the pier, slowly, looking at the high-powered yachts. Charlie Wilson was sitting on his deck. He waved as she passed him. There were crates on the pier. And then she saw Gallagher, barechested, wearing an old pair of jeans. Grunting, he bent and then lifted a crate, set it on the deck. His back was sunburned and oiled with his sweat.

"Hot," she said.

He turned, looked up from the crate, looked back at it.

"No so hot, really," she said. "I drove by your house. A For Sale sign was on it."

"It's sold." He stopped working, leaned against the rail. Lighting a cigarette, he studied her. "Freckles. You been out in the sun."

"Yeah. I took some time off. I sat on the beach." She shrugged. "We were pretty famous for a while."

"Yeah."

"You read the story?"

"Nope. You want a beer?"

"Well . . . I don't want to keep you from your work."

"I got time. This boat doesn't run on a schedule." He went down below.

She jumped to the deck. There were cartons all around her. The crate, she saw, held a television set. "Where you headed?" she called.

He laughed in the galley. "Nowhere but up." He appeared with a couple of bottles in his hand, and gave her one, sitting on the edge of a crate. She sat on the railing and looked at the cartons.

"We, uh, didn't leave you much, did we."

"Hell. I didn't have a lot here to begin with. A few

good friends"—he drank from the bottle—"but it ain't gonna kill me to lose any warehouse. Anyway, I started to figure it was time."

"For what?"

"I don't know. For some kind of change. Get a move on. I'm forty-seven years old, but I figure I got at least one move left."

"To where?"

He shrugged and looked out at the bay. "Did you know you can run north from here to the Hudson, clear up to Canada, all by inland waterways. Everybody else is heading south and west. I figure I'd try going north and east."

"What's there when you get there?"

"Friend. Got a friend owns a vineyard up there. Needs a partner. I think I'd kind of like that, you know? I mean, growin the stuff. Instead of just sellin the bottles."

"Wine?"

"Champagne."

"Oh. Are you going with Nicky?"

"Nope. Nicky got herself a pretty good job. Keener."

"What?"

"Keener got her the job. I figured I wouldn't make the classiest reference, things how they are, so I told her to go ask Keener for a reference."

She smiled. "You and Keener. I figured you kind of got together at the end."

Gallagher shrugged. "Anyway, he got her a job at the Bureau. I figure they're gonna be an item pretty soon."

"Oh."

"What's the matter?"

"Nothing. Just . . . somebody else I misjudged."

"Oh. Well, you're older and wiser now."

"Yeah. Three weeks."

"No. Light-years."

"Do you think so?"

He nodded. "Oh, yeah. I can see it."

She looked at the bay. "So you're going alone?"

"Ortega's coming with me."

"Oh."

"And when I'm settled . . . Hell, I don't know. I got a

call from my daughter last month. From New York. She was there for the summer and she read all that—well, all that stuff in the papers, and she called. I got a feeling she doesn't like France. And her mother's about to get married again and move to Colorado—"

"And she wants to live with you?"

"Yeah, I think. I think I'd like that."

"Mmm." Meg looked at the water again. "Yeah. I grew up in the country myself. Stockbridge. You know it?"

"Massachusetts."

"Yeah. *The Berkshire Eagle.* Circulation, fifteen thousand, six hundred and four. It was my first summer job. I was sixteen. Christ. I wonder if the *Eagle*'d have me back."

He looked up. "Feeling sorry for yourself?"

"A little. Why not? Nobody else is." She watched him; he sat in the sun, looking placid. "Michael? Do you think if we'd met another way—"

He shook his head. "There's no other way we would have met."

"I guess so." She felt the irony of that. Of everything. Of all the facts she'd gotten and the meanings she'd missed. "Listen," she said. "I know you think what I do is nothing, but it's not nothing. I just—I just did it badly. I really love what I do. There's this picture I have: people all over are busy, working, having fun, or just sleeping. And it's up to us to, well, watch out, you know? To keep track, and to tell them all what's going on. And without us . . . Oh, hell, I don't know. I just think if I do it, if I really do it right, it's like keeping a promise. You know what I mean?"

He nodded. "Are you working now?"

"You mean now? This minute?"

"No." He smiled. "I mean—"

"No. But I've got my resumé working. I'll find something. Hey, I got a fifty-grand offer."

"For what?"

"Someone wanted a book."

"About what?"

"You and me. The Inside Story."

"Yeah?" He looked at her. "Whole lot of bread."

"Yeah."

"You feel bad about turning it down?"

"How'd you know I did?"

"I told you. You've changed. I can see it."

"Oh. I'll find something, Michael."

"I know. You found yourself. The other part's easy."
He stood.

She said, "Well, you gotta get back to work."

He nodded, looked at her. She moved from the railing,
and he held her for a moment, kissing her lightly.

"Take care," she said lightly. "And have a good trip."

"I will. You too."

"I don't know where I'm going."

"Sure you do, Megan. Nowhere but up."

"Yeah," she said slowly. "Nowhere but up."

INDEX, MIAMI *CHRONICLE-NEWS*   Oct. 1–31

Diaz, Joseph A. See also Labor—Unions—International
Dockworker's union (IDU); Crime—Florida; Crime—
Nevada

Spokesman for Justice Dept in Washington denounces
handling of Diaz case by US Atty Elliot Rossen; ex-
onerates Quinn on bribery charge; assails the improper
reporting of the case; Michael A. Gallagher, cleared by
Quinn in Diaz abduction, linked to reporter on Chronicle-
News. (Oct. 4, 1:5)

US Atty Elliot Rossen resigns under pressure from
Justice Dept; claims he's "as much a victim as Diaz."
(Oct. 7, 1:3)

US Atty Harrison Quinn resigns from office over
Diaz scandal; plans to withdraw from mayoral race.
(Oct. 11, 1:3)

Sources close to the investigation report new leads in
Diaz abduction; informant identifies Jack Alexander and
Wm. R. Patrick, both of Nevada and both with connec-

tions to Frank Cavaletti, as Diaz abductors; FBI Agt Robert M. Keener refuses to comment. (Oct. 22, 1:6)

Jack Alexander and Wm. R. Patrick testify briefly at grand jury probe; "Close, no cigar yet," Keener announces, "but we'll wrap this; it's only a matter of time." (Oct. 30, 17:2)